CRITIQUING CASTE
Dalit Short Stories

CRITIQUING CASTE

Dalit Short Stories

Anirban Mridha

AUTHORSPRESS

Worldwide Circulation through Authorspress Global Network
First Published in 2022
by
Authorspress
Q-2A Hauz Khas Enclave, New Delhi-110 016 (India)
Phone: (0) 9818049852
E-mail: authorspressgroup@gmail.com
Website: www.authorspressbooks.com

Critiquing Caste: Dalit Short Stories
ISBN 978-93-5529-264-3

Printed in India at Thomson Press (India) Limited

"Those who grow up in darkness look better with the ornaments of darkness."

– Manohar Mouli Biswas

Contents

1
Introduction

In order to understand the Dalits' position in Indian society, it is important to understand the caste system (*varna vyavastha*). The caste system, which has dominated Indian society for over 3,000 years, was developed by the *Brahmins* (Hindu priests) to maintain their superiority over the less educated and less skilled. Over time, the caste system was formalised into four distinct classes (*varnas*). At the top of the hierarchy are the Brahmins, who are considered arbiters in matters of learning, teaching, and religion. Next in line are the *Kshatriyas,* who are warriors and administrators. The third category is *Vaisyas,* who belong to the artisan and commercial class. Finally, the *Sudras* (Backward Caste) are farmers and peasants. These four castes are socially and religiously important because they are said to have divine origination – they came from different parts of the Hindu god *Brahma,* the creator. The Brahmins came from the mouth of Brahma, the Kshatriyas from his arms, the Vaisyas from his thighs, and Sudras from his feet. Beneath the four classes, there is a fifth group, which is not included as part of the caste system. Individuals from this group are literally untouchable for the rest of the castes.

The *Dalits* (broken people) compose this untouchable society. The term "broken" has meant oppression for many radical Dalits who have used the term in their struggle for liberation. Gandhian liberals referred them as *Harijans* (children of god) and the Government of India officially calls them "Scheduled Castes." "Scheduled" means they are on a government schedule that entitles them to certain protections and affirmative action.

For centuries, Dalits were not treated as part of the mainstream Indian society, and they were traditionally assigned menial and degrading jobs. Some traditional roles, such as removing dead animals or playing drums at religious ceremonies, are expected to be carried out without compensation. Despite protections in the Indian Constitution, attempts by Dalits to be treated fairly in the workplace are often countered by violence and social or economic boycotts by the other castes.

Although the concept of untouchability was made illegal after India gained independence in 1947, the persecution and alienation of the Dalits has not stopped. In fact, it is reported to be at an all-time high. Entire villages in many Indian states are segregated by caste with the intent to keep Dalits away from higher castes. For example, it is common in many rural areas to have a designated area called "Dalit Street," which is the only place Dalits are allowed to live. Dalits typically live in locations more distant from village roads, an indication of segregation and a reminder of their untouchability.

Dalits are not allowed to fetch water from the same wells used by higher castes, visit the same temples, drink from the same cup at local tea shops, or claim land that is legally theirs. Dalit children who attend school must sit in the back of the classrooms. Moreover, the villages where Dalits live have limited or no access to public transportation, health care, or educational, political, or legal institutions.

Indian writing in English has flourished over the past two hundred years. A large variety of literature in English has been written in all the genres---poetry, drama, and fiction. The concerns of Indian English literature have similarly covered a very large area but it is noticeable that very few works of Indian short story in English have addressed the issue of the 'untouchables' in India. However, there have been exceptions and two major collections of short stories in translation, namely, *Poisoned Bread: Translations from Modern Marathi Dalit Literature* (edited by Arjun Dangle) and *Survival and Other Stories: Bangla Dalit Fiction in Translation* (edited by

Sankar Prasad Singha and Indranil Acharya) speak of Dalit lives lived on the edge and of suffering, negation and revolt. It will be the major objective of this book to look at the spectrum of experiences as depicted in these probing and absorbing stories.

Traditionally, Indian literature has either ignored untouchables or portrayed them as victims in need of saviours, or as objects without voice or agency. The two collections of short stories to be studied in detail, however, do not quite fit into this paradigm since all of them tell stories of the lives of untouchable men and women bearing witness to the oppression and exploitation as members of stigmatised and oppressed communities.

The stories in *Poisoned Bread* forcefully convey the 'differentness' of Dalit literature. There is a big hiatus between the prose of Marathi literature and that of Dalit literature. It is immediately recognised that the language, experience and heroes of Dalit literature are totally different. In selecting stories the quality of writing has been the main criterion. Another has been the aim of showing the material and psychological situation of the Dalits living in urban slums, those living in rural areas, are those who have risen to the middle class through special facilities for their castes. The heroes of these stories are shown confronting limitations, abject poverty, misery and brutality. In the stories '*Gold from the Grave*', '*Mother*' and '*Livelihood*' is depicted fierce battle for life in an urban slum, and a world surviving beyond the pale of so called 'cultural values'. '*The Poisoned Bread*', '*The Cult*', '*The Refugee*', '*Explosion*', '*The Storeyed House*' demonstrate the position of the Dalits in rural society, and their fight for existence. '*The Storeyed House*' gives a glimpse of how Dalits wishing to live honourably with respect, on terms of equality are presented by higher castes. If this story shows attitudes of caste superiority, then '*Promotion*' reveals the ambivalent crisis of identity of Dalit middle class.

Bandhumadhav's *Poisoned Bread* is all about the inhuman treatment of a human being who earns 'poisoned bread' with a long day's hard toil. The 'killing' of the grandfather by the Patil triggers off the anger of the grandson and leaves him with a sense of fury and disgust, prompting him to retaliate.

Waman Hoval's *The Storeyed House* portrays how the aspiration of an old retired dockyard worker Bayaji to build a storeyed house of his own and to live happily with his eight kids together gets abandoned by the jealousy of his social 'superior' Kondiba Patil. Though Bayaji was forced to take up the conventional three-portioned house he failed to quench Kondiba's thirst for 'revenge' (There was only one storeyed house in the village and that belonged to Kondiba). Kondiba along with Bhujaba and a few other seasoned rascals of the village burn down the house along with Bayaji on the day of the traditional housewarming ceremony.

Yogiraj Waghmare's *Explosion* brings out the pain and suffering of an educated Mahar young man, Shetiba who is dragged into scavenging because of a poor socio-economic condition.

Arjun Dangle's *Promotion* brilliantly portrays the plight of a newly promoted officer of the reserved category who helplessly and selfishly too is trying to get rid of his low-origin but is reminded by people around him that he belongs, after all to the realm of the 'untouchables'. His supposed superiority gets frustrated after his son gets beaten up by a high-born old woman for touching her water pot.

Baburao Bagul's *Mother* brings out the helplessness of two beings – a mother and a son. Despite their great efforts to live for each other they get defeated in the hands of a cruel world--- the son becomes a monstrous reflection of the father to the mother and the mother becomes a selfish greedy whore to the son.

Amitabh's *The Cull* gives a surrealistic picture of a Mahar's shanty town where a few many hungry 'human beings' are seen to fight the crows and dogs and vultures to have their share of meat.

Keshav Meshram's *Barriers* can well serve as an eye-opener to all those who love to play with fire. The low-born young lad Narayan had to face humiliation at every step--- a dog can quench its thirst at will but not he, urine of cow got spread on things he touched, he had to drink water from the aluminium pot which his Headmaster's 'keep' used for her ablutions after relieving herself, he was deprived of the school to work as a bonded labourer in the Headmaster's house where food was thrown to him from above after his hard work in the well from morning to night, his friend was scolded by his father simply because he treated him as a human being, despite his great sportsmanship he was not allowed to participate in the sports meet, his killing was planned by his Headmaster because he dared to distribute 'jalebis' and that the Headmaster had to eat it. The only answer Narayan could think of giving to the monstrosity of this society--- he set on fire the house of the Head master along with him and his mistress.

Anna Bhau Sathe's *Gold from the Grave* is the pitiful record of gigantic man, Bheema, who, despite his great strength and courage had to make a living on the gold ornaments left with the rich corpses. The story culminates in a great fight between Bheema and the jackals for the possession of a carcass, which, of course, ends with Bheema losing one finger.

Avinash Dolas *The Refugee* is an account of a young man who had to leave everything---his father, his mother, his brother, his village simply because he protested against the high-caste people who ordered all the Mahars to empty a well from where a low-caste woman has drawn water.

Survival and Other Stories is a collection of translated dalit stories primarily based on an anthology of Bangla stories, published in 1996, entitled *Chaturtha Duniyar Galpo* (Stories of the Fourth World). The Bengali anthology was a compilation of stories published in the quarterly Chaturtha Duniya. It was jointly edited by Achintya Biswas, Manohar Mouli Biswas and Kapil Krishna Thakur. The stories are richly varied in the choice of locale, theme and characters. The common feature of all the stories is the representation of a hitherto neglected populace and its ways of life. The traditional cultural ethos as embodied in the mainstream Bengali literature is a thousand miles apart from these tales of exploitation and sorrow. The authentic Dalit consciousness is revealed in these stories which show the three most important features of Dalit literature – suffering, revolt and negation. The truth of representation is entirely a discourse of social progress and development in the late twentieth century and the early twenty-first century with a critical eye. Even the portrayal of the downtrodden in the writings of Sarat Chandra and Bibhuti Bhushan may seem inadequate vis-à-vis the acutely realistic delineation of Dalit sensibility in these narratives.

Gobindo Shoundo's story *Jale Dangai* (On Water and on Shore) is a sad tale of a poor fisherman, Shashi, who gets stuck in a tempest during his routine trip to the sea in search of fish. At one point of time, he has to witness in a helpless manner the loss of his elder son in the strong current. The portrayal of this harsh struggle for survival in the deep recesses of the violent sea can perhaps not be authentically done merely by virtue of literary imagination. It demands first-hand experiences of the brutal caprices of marine life. It also narrates the vicious cycle of debt in which moneylenders trap these poor fishermen. The power relation in the lowest rungs of society is so heavily one-sided that the mainstream myth of progress seems a distant dream to these hapless social marginals.

Makhanlal Pradhan's *Gopal Chashir Jat Dharma* (Farmer Gopal's Caste and Creed) is a moving tale of a Dalit farmer who has to try his luck in different profession in search of his livelihood. Driven out of his family occupation of agriculture owing to the extreme greed of land sharks ready to change the skyline of the suburbs of Kolkata with high-rises, he is reduced to a bonded labourer with a paltry earning. Any dream of prosperity eludes him and he is forced to carry on an ignominious life without any hope of betterment.

Kapil Krishna Thakur's *Anya Ihudi* (The Other Jew) manifests the helplessness of a large number of refugee Bengali families who were driven out of erstwhile East Pakistan during and after partition. In India they are treated like Dalits; even their religious affiliation to the major Hindu community fails to protect them from the anti-socials. In this way, they are doubly victimised by the major religious community – Muslims in East Pakistan and Hindus in India.

Goutam Ali's *Haat* (Market Place, translated as Bazaar) is a poignant portrayal of 'sexploitation' that dalitises women of lower classes in the most ignominious way. The dark underbelly of the modern urban apartment culture has been ruthlessly exposed by the writer with the description of the sickening commodification of the female body. The discourse of dalitisation takes a curious turn when the sexual aberrations of the middle-aged husband are silently approved by the ailing, almost invalid wife.

Shyamal Kumar Pramanik's *Ekhono Adim* (Survival) proclaims the invincibility of Dalit consciousness reflected in literature. The author creates the ambience of a general thriller when he projects the indomitable courage of a food grain collector whose family would starve to death if he is unable to collect grains from the snake's lair. Death looms large over the ordeal of life, and survival is ensured after a close encounter with a venomous serpent.

Manoranjan Barman's *Shabori* (literally, huntress, here referring to a woman belonging to the lowly Shabor caste) highlights the different standpoints of the two protagonists---Padma and Rekha. It skilfully depicts, on the one hand, the sufferings of a metropolitan woman arising out of sudden loss of her husband's job, and on the other, it draws an inspiring image of a rustic woman, Padma, whose misfortune fails to throttle her inexhaustible life force. The story handles a larger-than-life thematic canvas that could perhaps have been expanded into a novel.

Achinta Biswas's *Bipralabdha* (the deceived) busts the myth of development by exposing the shabby treatment of dalit people by the administration and policy makers. The story not only concerns itself with untouchability in West Bengal but also highlights the discriminatory distribution of civic amenities.

Susnata Jana's *Mahashweta Gramer Mukunda Ebong Ek Ascharjo Pronoy* (Mukunda and an Extraordinary Love Affair) has captured the socio-economic parameters that have throttled the egalitarian voices in this caste-ridden society despite the psychological transformation in the young representatives of the new generations – both upper and lower classes.

Sunil Kumar Das's *Dhani Bauri Ganga Pelo* (Dhani Bauri Gets 'Salvation') is quite unconventional in its attempt to portray the hierarchy amongst various dalit communities. Ironically, the 'greater' Dalit, a female employee in Coal India, contributes her earning for the welfare of the 'lesser' dalit family. Still, she is looked down upon by the daughter-in-law of that family as an untouchable, impure woman.

Anil Gharai's *Punascha Parashuram* (Reincarnation of Parashuram) cleverly exploits the Parashuram myth when an old dalit mother is hacked to death by her own son who gets entrapped by a gunin (witch doctor).

Nalini Bera's *Bara Bhaja, Kata Chokh o Badhuker Galpo* (The Story of the Grey-eyed Oil-fry Seller) shows that the various vices that corrupt mainstream society are emphatically present in the marginalised world of dalit people. The theme of ingratitude and betrayal becomes quite apparent in the evolving relationship of Parva, the mother surrogate, and Bankim Badhuk, an ingrateful wretch.

Taraknath Majhi's *Sakhya* (Friendship) skilfully arranges the sequence of numerous political strifes and conflicts in the Gangetic plains of West Bengal. The people of a lower social strata have gradually disappeared as the outcome of such political tussles of power.

Manohar Mouli Biswas's *Munnali* is a touching tale of an individual who is cruelly reminded of the insurmountable social barrier even in modern times.

Nakul Mallick's *Chashar Beta* (The Son of a Peasant) dares to treat a social 'superior' as a slave and sends a strong message of reversal in the movement of the caste-ridden social juggernaut as a low-caste zamindar harnesses an upper-caste zamindar in place of an ox for ploughing his land.

It is apparent that Dalit narratives are *narratives of pain* and it is *pain* which strings one narrative event to the next, and it is *pain* that binds individual Dalits together into an 'imagined community' of fellow sufferers. Yet the experience of oppression does not imprison Dalits in eternal victim-hood. In all the stories the Dalits are represented standing against the cruel and inhuman social orders born of caste-based discrimination.

2

Poisoned Bread: Translations from Modern Marathi Dalit Literature

Bandhumadhav's *Poisoned Bread*

Bandhumadhav, the author not only portrays the common Dalit scene in Maharashtra but he also scorns and slaps from a much logical viewpoint in his Poisoned Bread. Devoid of land rights the lives of Mahars walk through a path of infectious agony and never get to make a statement out of the strangulated voices. The story, conceived in the year of 1992, bares the horrific picture of the miserable livelihoods 'the oppressed' have to live under the forceful domination of Bramhins and other upper caste Hindus.

The story begins with the narrator's nostalgic reminiscence at the time of coming harvest, watching the birds whirling in the sky. The anguish that burns every 'Dalit' beneath their flesh rises in the form of printed letters as the narrator exclaims: "my heart bleeds like a wounded bird". Keeping resemblance with the birds or carving the agony on words – whichever be the motive, the line brings out the puss staggered for centuries.

The narrator walks down his memory lane and stoops near a piece of grief stuck in his throat – a twelve-year-old harvest. Bandhumadhav portrayed three different and distinct characters in Poisoned Bread: the narrator, his grandfather Yetala and the land owner Patil. Yetala and Patil create the cycle of dominated and dominant. Patils have been dominating and tormenting the lives of Mahars and Mangs for years. They have helped the communal discrimination grow to the point of a stalemate trap – a dead end.

Safron politics is a form that lashes over the urban society with its orthodox bramhinist solicitations. But Bandhumadhav reaches the root level to conceive the story and looks for a remedy for the receiving end. Education might have been the instant remedy for the oppressed but the retarded religious prejudices have castled the bramhinists from all the rational arguments. Patil's words come from a sense of right and possession over the act of racial domination and sense of higher hierarchy. On the other hand, Yetala apparently is meek and seems to have accepted the fact that they are to be dominated and trampled. He detests the position he is given and deep down he definitely is at war against the racial discrimination but fail to demand equality under the gripping claw of aging. With the time the protesting voice has eroded and has become a gibberish shrill exclaiming the failing rebellion. Yetala falters and kneels before Patil several times in order to keep him from infuriating and ends up beneath the boots. The narrator here brings in the voice of rationality and retorts and argues with Patil unknowing the fact that it's futile to convince a vegetated conscience that's been holding on to the flawed sense of superiority for thousands of years. The narrator strikes against the pliability of Yetala who's submitted to his destiny of being dominated: "I am your slave...I am your begging Mahar and feel proud to be so" (Yetala). They have now been impervious to the insolence and abuse and pain inflicted by the so-called higher community.

Bandhumadhav directly questions the concept of position imposed by the power-hungry Bramhinists. Whilst educational qualification and advanced modern rationality are being suppressed by the stalemate convention the narrator retorts with an enraged flame. A simple belief, as we all are taught since childhood, is that it's a respectful and submissive gesture if you hold something against your head. But it is literally unethical and disrespectful if you touch something with your feet (books, Prasad and other things or so). Now the question arises: who's made this discrimination between the head and feet and if made, why? Both of them are fellow parts of our bodies. If some deist claims that we all are created by the same God, then why has He created such sinful organs? The same question has been conceived in the story. Patil claims, "...the rain-god got enraged because of you – the Mahars and Mangs – have profaned religion, and abandoning caste, have defiled Lord Vithoba of Pandharpur..." Now if the holy God has created us then how hypocritical He is to create such denigrating creatures! The scorn is accompanied with a revolting strike as Mhadeva, the narrator fires back: "...if a religion can't tolerate one human being treating another simply as a human being, what's the use of such inhumane religion?"

All the arguments and logics were turned down by one optimal solution provided by the bourgeois Bramhinist: how much should a Mahar be educated or qualified he must always remain under the feet of the communal 'superiors' and be labelled as 'chappal'. The story progresses to describe the unspeakable distress and torture people like Yetala receive. Fear threatens and poverty seals their lips. Poverty, unemployment and throttled hopes lash on their torso time and again. As long as the narrator claims his rightful equality Patil keeps coiling up with murderous rage. The humiliation continues all along when they work in the field. Yetala after getting deprived of his fair share of Jowar for the day despite all his begging, finally urges to take home some stale mouldering crumbs smeared with dung and urine which had turned green and foul and were rejected by oxen. The pathetic scenery exhibits the desperation of 'Dalits' fastened in land-bondage. The narrator with his rebellious character tries to convince his grandfather to finally charge a defiance against the prolonged suffering.

It's pretty optimistic and heart-warming to talk or dream about a revolt but the asphyxiating reality buries them all with its grim shovel. The food that was not meant for anybody to eat, not even for animals, was consumed by Yetala at night out of the fuming hunger in his aging stomach. 'Hard kick in the loins' – that's what they 'deserved' and their rightful share of humiliation ends in Yetala's death-death, handed by that stale rotten bread.

The heart wrenching part of the story comes at the climax where Yetala mumbles his last words to the narrator. Along with the sounds of loud wailings, hopeless mourning and shrills of ominous lapwings Yetala in his frail voice tells the narrator never to depend on the age-old bread associated with their caste. 'Take away this accursed bread from the mouths of the Mahars' is the line where he blesses his grandchild to get free from the curse of being dominated by social and racial discrimination.

The bread for Mahars, Dalits has always been poisoned with insolence from Bramhinist feudal. It has been, very much like the crumbs, smeared with the urine of shear humiliation that has been conceived as a birth right by upper caste Hindus all over India. The discrimination and dominance along with distress pierce them for centuries. They writhe in pain until they die. But sometimes the pain stacks inside and turns into a farness and inflames people like narrator with rage and disgust, prompting them to retaliate. The title itself slaps every reader in the face and bares in front of them the horrific face of reality. The line that remains after the story ends like an echoing refrain is: "This poisonous bread will finally kill the very humanness of man. . . "

Waman Hoval's *The Storeyed House*

After Ambedkar converted himself to a Buddhist in order to imply his defiance against Hindu beliefs and casteism, on 4th October, 1956 (publicly), a handsome number of his followers (Ambedkarites) also followed his path. Under the lead of Surai Sasai the conversion took shape in 1966. With the twenty-two vows of Ambedkar they had forbidden Hindu gods and culture but still are not treated any better than before even in today's scenario. The clearly went for refuge but have been interpreted and branded as anti-Hindus as the leaders of dalit Bahujan Samaj Party claim. Before all the criticism it is to be clarified that turning into Buddhists made no big difference for them. The upper caste Hindus still continue to humiliate them mentioning the fact that their precursors were lower caste Hindus or Shudras.

The story by Waman Hoval – *The Storeyed House* conceives the same concept of never-ending discrimination. Bayaji, who had turned a Buddhist was a worker in Mumbai docks for years and at the end of his prolonged service had earned a fair amount of money. The story revolves around Bayaji and his sons and the dominating influence they all have to suffer in the hands of the local influential Bramhin. Their dreams were demolished as the Bramhinist society doesn't want them grow to the equal level of prosperity.

The story starts with Bayaji's arrival as he travels by a State Transport bus to his village. The heckling journey of Bayaji and the condition of the bus ironically mocks the present state of Hindu society and political immobility in India. The author here creates a garrulous tone with his rhetorical approach while describing the journey. As the author indirectly directs the immobile social and racial beliefs the whole thing contains a stint of black humour.

There is a character named Bhujaba, a known rascal who is associated with the influential bureaucrat, Patil. Bhujaba, at first greets Bayaji as a respected aged but as he doesn't get greeted back as he expected he fumes up. Bayaji is reminded once again about his forefathers belonging to Dalit or Achchut community. He used to be a Mahar. And, the upper castes won't stop discriminating completely disregarding the fact that he no longer belongs to Hindu community. Well, that being said, the only dignity remains for him in the society is locked inside his suitcase, the life-long earning of his (though he never held a high designation).

Prosperity has always been the prime discriminating factor in capitalist society. Bayaji could not be touched as long as he had the handsome amount of money. With that money, he wished to build a house for his family – a storeyed house. But it was Kondiba Patil who interpreted Bayaji's approach as a retort towards his pride as he only had a two storeyed house in the village. "Do you aspire to an equal status with us by building this house?" – this statement by Kondiba clarifies the whole picture. "They are forgetting their place" is the sense that twists their stomach as the intend to dominate the Dalit community for good.

They story tells of a journey to solidify a dream against the dominance and humiliation of Bramhinist society. Although Bayaji had to build the house with a concealed staircase and upper storey, although his dreams were burnt to ashes, his dreams raised an uproar against the domination. The ceremony of house-opening depicts the beautiful traditions and cultures of his community. Bayaji was pressurised by Kondiba and finally his house was burnt along with his body.

Bayaji's family and his sons represent the beauty of a rural and not-so-high earning family. The determination and genuineness of his eldest son definitely leaves a mark. After the death of Bayaji he carries on the protest that his father started inadvertedly and goes on to fulfill his father's dreams.

The creation – the foundation of Bayaji might have turned into ashes but his dreams of establishing their dignity-existence and solidifying equal rights for Dalits had survived and, fueled by the strong wills of his eldest son created an optimistic flame that would one day secure, certainly a better life for not only converted Mahars but also every dalit in the country. "We are starting on a house, not with a concealed first floor but a regular two-storeyed house." Hereby the eldest son renounces the resurrection of his father's dreams and the author concludes the story on a positive note.

There was no explosive outburst in the story but there was a composed movement, a silent and gracious one, formed with dreams of emancipation and humanity of a 'man'.

Yogiraj Waghmare's *Explosion*

Explosion, the title tells of something that's anticipated. The anguish, the void and the rage stacked for centuries inside pale hearts of a community eagerly wait to explode. The *Explosion* is not only anticipated but also needed right now. The authoritarian domination that they have faced for centuries must have to be repelled at a certain point of time and perhaps the time is now. In Bandhumadhav's short story Poisoned Bread old Yetala urges to his grandson to abandon the cursed livelihood, their profession of being trampled. The land rights were not something very familiar for the Dalit community in the villages of Maharashtra (not to mention, Uttar Pradesh also). Here in his story Yogiraj creates a field of high frequency where emotions have overwritten the plot. The plot is a simple one revolving around Sheku and his son Shetiba. The author portrays the relation of father and son on the background of a family that lives hand to mouth. More importantly he creates a heavy emotional ride through straight notes of sentiment and concern. Then comes the *Explosion* right at the end of the story with one single line of Shetiba's letter. Defiance is something that is to be shown or hoisted but refusal is much more of a rebellion and refusal that is to be conceived in the core of the heart. Tears, blood, humiliation and everything that comes for a Mahar or Mang with his surname, have to be refused to receive. The decisions taken by sheku and Shetiba don't define the *Explosion* as it was a silent one but was more impactful than a thousand Morchas.

Now, let's concentrate on the character portraits. Sheku is an old and concerned father who has now in no shape to face the toil of the field. He has to face the poverty of his family with tied hands. He sold his share of land with a deep belief in his son's capability to earn bread for the whole family. But the present situation puts them in a microeconomic devastation. His son, Shetiba, though passing the matriculation examination has been still yet to find a job to feed his family. Evidently, the Oppressed have been deprived from their rights since long. Manuvadis still treat them like untouchables and the scope for education or job is very narrow on the scenario. In this kind of socio-economical condition it wasn't that intriguing that Shetiba couldn't secure a decent job.

The story begins with Sheku waiting for his son to return who has gone in search of a job at the factory of Dhoki. Relieving his father's concerns Shetiba returns home but with empty hands. The ambience created by the author here in Sheku's home is pretty dim and oppressed according to the mental state of the characters. Sheku in great anxiety asks his son about his job and as usual the answer comes, 'no'. The grave tension brewing inside all the timid hearts condenses with the darkness. The existence of racial discrimination shows up its surreal face as Shetiba startles hearing the word 'Saheb'. Shetiba was one of the few educated in his community; so, that makes sense how heavy expectations he had to bear on his back. His experience at the factory of Dhoki was sickening with the sight of people bearing molasses, covered in dirt.

After Shetiba's numerous failed attempts to secure a job Sheku with failing faith and disappointment decides to ask back his share of land. Sheku intended to send Shetiba back to the profession from which he wished to get rid of. Here starts the build to the *Explosion* that was to come. Shetiba vehemently opposed the decision of his father with all the silence of his heart.

He would rather go on to carry molasses than going back to the ancestral profession that had them dominated for a long time. With his explosive silence and repelling tears Shetiba raises his voice against the humiliation. As mentioned before, it is more defying when you refuse to the trampling than to walk on a rally ceremoniously hoisted by false activists. Ritwik Ghatak, the revolutionary film director exclaimed once, "Everything's burning! The universe is burning! And, so am I!" That same physical and psychological burning that has been turning the Oppressed into ashes for centuries now turns into the most silent of screams that pierces a hole into that impasse wall of discrimination. Even after the story ends that mumbling, "Father please don't do this to me" echoes like a plangent murmur.

Arjun Dangle's *Promotion*

With the title of the story being conceived so ironically it was evident that the story itself will exceptionally satirise the bigger picture. The story differs in its own rights from most others stories in this collection by Arjun Dangle. Dangle proves his prominence as the one of the leading names in Dalit literature. The story has a firm build on the background of a family that has shortly risen to a comfortable economic status and has stepped duly into urban lifestyle.

Waghmare, the protagonist, certainly does not resemble a rebellious hero or a rising voice. Instead, Waghmare reminds of the crow in disguise of a peacock; only on a higher and more serious scale. There has been many an instance in Indian literature where an act of disowning has been described. It's a sense of shame that leads people to disown their own origin and it's the shame that has been questioned by Dangle in the story. Similarly, there used to be a class of people in British-ruled India who conceived western traditions in order to flatter the British empire only to get humiliated finally by their (the British's) unaltered sense of discrimination. They were still treated as slaves as we find in the short story 'Karma' by Khushwant Singh.

The story begins with a bit of an altercation between Waghmare and Godbole. Godbole is senior than Waghmare but inferior in designation as Waghmare was promoted to 'Sahib' before him. A professional jealousy and racial heat buzzes underneath the whole conversation. Dangle has portrayed the character of Waghmare with careful detailing. When he sits in his cabin and reassesses his intention of filing a case against Godbole, the frail and timid side of his character peeps underneath his achievements. He prepares the proposal himself instead of compelling that unwilling stuff of his to do it. The complex about his community overpowers his decisions and instincts. His ego overpowers both his id and super ego. His instincts writhe like a caged bird where his moralities have been blindfolded by force.

Every literary character needs a contrasting figure to flourish itself. In the story Awale plays the role of that contrasting figure. Awale vehemently opposes the thoughts and actions of Waghmare. Waghmare belonging to the oppressed community had been promoted under 33% reservation category. But it's isn't an obliging act for the authority to promote him; moreover, it's something he has proved himself worthy of and has every right to hold the position. It wasn't much years ago, when the oppressed were not given the opportunity to be called 'Saheb' or to hold such a dignified designation. "But remember these other people have enjoyed 100% reserved category for centuries" – this line obviously is an instance of Awale's disgust as he means to establish the fact that the other castes and communities have been privileged for ages, depriving them from their human rights. Awale's roaring voice against social discrimination startles Waghmare but he, on every occasion sidesteps them with great care. He declines Awale's proposal to print the receipt books for Backward Class Workers. He even avoids attending the Association's meetings in order to avoid 'unnecessary problems'. There could be two cases here with the protagonist: 1) He's too obliged to the 'authority' for his position that he righteously doesn't go against them to ask for the rights of his own people. He doesn't want to offend them in any circumstances. And, 2) He hypocritically wants to feign his identity as he himself now looks upon his people as the backward class, the faltered class.

His show of interest in Sai Baba Shirdi fails to veil his flawed, spineless mentality. Waghmare's hypocrisy starts turning more distinct when he boards the train. All his activities point towards his complex and intention of disguising himself as someone he's not. He disowns his origin in order to avoid the humiliation that has tailed them for centuries now. He's concerned about his fellow commuter's acknowledgement about his caste. He intends to change his surname as it's something that proves him to be inferior. His inertia directs towards his lacking sense of equality. All of the castes that are divided by the misinterpretation of 'Varnashrama', are equals as human beings and there is absolutely nothing to be ashamed of if someone is a scheduled caste or so (if it's judged from a rational viewpoint obviously). But the upper caste communities still treat the oppressed like inferiors following up with shear humiliation and that's something that helps growing the complex Waghmare conceives.

His disgustful reaction towards his wife's poor relative (who resides in a slum) clarifies the whole picture and his consciousness about his acquired 'status'. "Learn to maintain your status. After all, you're an officer's wife." But all his sense of 'high status' shatters into pieces as soon as he learns how the upper castes still treat them from none other than his own son. The treatment for the

'Achchut' has remained the same. The Hindu society hasn't yet changed their ways of treating the oppressed. Communal discrimination still remains with its stinging presence. And, that is the 'abyss' Dangle mentions in the conclusion of the story.

The character of Waghmare inadvertently serves the means of racial discrimination. The climax of the story can be judged as a cathartic ending for Waghmare or a tragic end to his pride and act of disowning as he got stuck between his pride and conscience.

Baburao Bagul's *Mother*

The title of the story could be a bit deceiving and at the same time pretty fitting too. The word 'mother' beholds a vast perception and an eternal collaboration of the most primitive emotions. It makes no difference between a Hindu and a Muslim, an oppressed and a privileged, a human being and a wild animal when it comes to motherly emotion. Baburao Bagul, the author, has woven the story so beautifully that it has reached the status to be a perfect short story. Between a sudden beginning and an abrupt ending lies an impressive emotional rollercoaster. The story conceives a simple plot and complex but instinctive perspectives accompanied by a consistent tone of pensive partings. *Mother* is the aura that circulates the story and emotions have wheels. Emotions change and turn in order to provide the story with stinging realism. Obviously, the story is written on the 'untouchable' background as both the protagonist and the true antagonist breathe in that accursed ambience. What overlaps the background completely is the relation between the widow and her son. The treatment and position and adversities that a young single mother has to face in the lower tier of the society have been portrayed with horrifying clarity. The characters act according to their Eros tells them to. There isn't much of a scope for super ego to get involved with their respective psyches. Morality stands afar and the characters go on to become the puppets of their own instincts and instantaneous impulses.

There are some distinct characters to talk about. If we just put aside the central characters we shall be left with a bullying system, a lustful buzzard of a man, a sick and frail husband imprisoned inside his complex and suspicion and a lustful, forceful overseer who shackles his prey with his sexuality. And, above all there is the denigrating pair of eyes owned by frivolous society.

Pandu is the young introvert protagonist who has learnt about the stings and venoms of this society in a very young age. As he continues to writhe in excruciating pain inflicted by his surrounding and community a futile but combustible rage brews inside his little heart. His tortured abstinence fumes up in revenge but his defiance is overpowered by his insecure being. Though all the travesties he's still a kid who craves for his mother's affection and care. His actions are motivated by his rush of emotions only.

On the other hand, Pandu's mother who has been a widow for ten long years has finally found a pair of strong masculine arms to relieve herself. In the story, she has no name and that's because she's just as same as all the women in the world. This is a universal story of every single mother. Besides being a mother, a single mother, to be more specific, she's a woman und a beautiful one. She has her youth and the intoxicating sex-drive. Just like all the creatures she has her sexuality, her thirst for love. It's certainly not licentious if a woman who has been starving for a decade satisfies her craving with her overseer. And, it certainly does not make her a whore if she has that alluring appeal and a body to lust for. Not only that, she has all the motherly attributes and has sacrificed her luxury for her child. She has been loyal to every duty she has towards her child. She has battled all along against the society she lives in to protect her child from all the malice. Now she has found the way to her rejuvenation through the overseer and has managed to earn a significant amount. While going through all these she hasn't been able to manage a fair amount of time for her son in the process. Now this is the situation that the story breathes in.

The story starts in Pandu's school where they were being taught a poem on motherhood. The running emotions had loosened Pandu's sentiments from their usual erect. He was responding to his circumference. He smiled for the first time and its unusual sight caught the attention of his classmates. Child can be the most savage being at times because they not knowing much about what they're speaking about emphasise on the speaking itself. His classmates' parents often made a gossip about his single mother and envious of her youth often labelled her a 'whore'. The pupil near abstinence mocked him with that very word and the expressions imitating a prostitute near her orgasm. They called him a pimp and thrashed upon him with other venomous abuses. A futile rage and a lump of tears reddened his childish eyes and his tormented soul literally begged for blood. He turned into a murderer, not by his deeds but by his thoughts inside his brain. In his head, he had killed several of those who carried on making obnoxious gestures pointing to his loving mother. It was humiliation at its prime for a kid of that age.

The humiliation didn't end here for Pandu. He had gone through the indifference and negligence of his mother towards him for months. On his way back to home his blood was fuming up right to his head and he could barely manage himself from recoiling at those boys who abused him. After reaching home his eyes daunted with hunger found no edible food in the kitchen. His mother's negligence was proved to him as he recalled her reluctant behaviour from previous night. Dagdu was their neighbour who heavily lusted upon the expressive youth of his mother as usual kept calling her bad names in his vitriol madness. The abuse against his mother this time had some kind of positive effect on Pandu's current situation. The abused not only sympathised with him but also fuelled his growing suspicion about his mother's occupation. It's the society that creates this miscommunication even between son and his mother. Pandu was vulnerable indeed because he literally had nobody in the world except his mother. It wasn't his fault that he had started to fall in the trap of the society. The socials create morals out of their own agendas. Dagdu abused her because he didn't get to enjoy her youth – her 'delicious' body. The women in the community abuse her because their husbands often bare her with their filthy stares when she passes. It's a hard womanly envy that leads them to abuse her. The boys in the school abuse her because their parents do – because the community does. Pandu's

TB-infected father used to abuse her out of his nasty suspicion and complex. His suspicion-ridden eyes humiliated her by checking every part of her body, the private parts too. She definitely has done injustice with her son by that negligence. But it wasn't her fault completely. It was the overseer who didn't let her loose. He spared her no time when she could be with her son. With lustful arms he grasped her days fulfilling his physical craving. She was starving for ten long years and it was very natural and instinctive to wallow into the intoxicating vessel. So, she was emotionally and sexually vulnerable too and ultimately the society took this advantage to fulfil its agendas.

When she returned home there were neighbours surrounding her threshold as Pandu was weeping sitting there. She then somehow saw the shadow of her deceased husband in Pandu. The incident led her to go back in her memories of her husband who used to suspect her for extramarital affairs and tortured and abused her. She at that moment cursed her child incidentally. But the reality knocked her door open when poor Pandu unable to hold his sobs and insecurity back cried out piteously. She then realised how vulnerable and helpless her son is without her. Pandu's insecurity melted away when his mother hugged him and adored him with her care, new clothes and food. But those things of amour had a repulsive effect as his suspicion wasn't removed. The viewpoint and frivolity of the society is depicted at the line: "Your mother's business...big rush...five rupees for each customer..." It was stated by the boys in his colony when he wore new shirt on previous Diwali. A gift of love from a mother was intentionally interpreted by the society as something bought by a profitable prostitute. That darkness had stamped Pandu's immature mind with its dark grim claw. Those memories haunted him only to make him yell to his mother: "Whore! I spit on your clothes" and run away from home. And, with that line he made the cruel devilish society triumph. The community was successful turning him against his mother. His mother's heart shattered into pieces and he was thrown into the doom of insecurity.

She held herself guilty and still waited for her son to return. When there was a knock at the door her emotions rushed towards it expecting his son's return. But it was her overseer instead who at once fastened her with his strong lusty arms feigning the support and comfort. Her son returned at the moment she was embraced (groped) by her lover. Pandu's suspicion completely turned into belief. It was a disease that was injected into his flawless childish heart by the crooked society. He was made to misinterpret his loving mother for her she had once fought against the community. He turned against the woman who sacrificed her every luxury, her needs and rejected many a rich man who lusted for her with their bulky pockets. The story ended abruptly with a numb void and rage towards the social treatment and detestable perspectives. None of the mother and son can be blamed for the tragic end. They acted by their instincts and were justified at their respective viewpoints. The only one to blame is the society that they reside in. And the last line tells it all: "she found release impossible..." The society had created an impasse for the women and that impasse is still tearing them apart.

Amitabh's *The Cull*

Human race is a civilised one as it's claimed. But the primitive instincts still live inside the psyche though submerged. In the prehistoric age when human wasn't the race that claimed to be intellectually superior and 'civilised' it was a war between men and the beasts to gain possession over the food. When that war was over and there was peace to set in men started a battle against one another. Then there were walls created between races and then the wall turned the society into separate pieces of socio-economic provinces gradually. The Indian society although being rich in culture and creed had its own discriminations. And that same discrimination, casteism, racial and communal oppression turned men again to that beast that they once used to be. The story '*The Cull*' portrays something very ominously real in a gory way. The ugly truth has been spoken through the short story by Amithabh. The title tells of the killing of a beast as a sacrificial custom.

The story begins at a shout spreading throughout the shanty town. The community of oppressed are delighted to hear the news of a cull. A holy cow has been culled and it would be their source of food for next few days. The altitude of poverty and its horrific face comes to sight at the beginning. The people would secure their meal from a dead animal – the thought itself is something not very sober. The whole village, all the people rush for their share of food. It's not something anyone reserves. They all have to race in order to save their respective lives. They all have to scratch and claw to have their household run for a few days. The microeconomic condition clearly depicts the wretched face of the whole Mahar community in of Maharashtra. As Charles Darwin wrote in his 'Origins of Life' it was truly the 'survival of the fittest'. Pandya and his son were dragging the corpse of the cow as they were seen by Bulkai who informed the others in the town. The news spread like a wildfire as the only tyrant in the town was hunger itself.

Everyone with buckets, knives and troughs rushes towards the gum trees where the corpse of the cow was hung. The intelligent and exerting ones reached earlier to the spot to claim their share at first. Vithi who had a large brood to feed hurried her son up from bed. Her husband was asthmatic and she had three sons. She wasn't able to go and collect the meat and so she sent her son Nilya to the spot. Underage Nilya had to run in the race to food with sleep dripping from his eyelids.

The battle for food had begun already. Pandya with his son skinned the cow and claimed their deserving share of meat. Nobody could touch the carcass before he completed his job. Drenched in blood he did his work neatly and the others around were too had their clothes stained. Pandu and his son Soumya wedged the carcass between the gum trees and slashed their favorable pieces of meat. Old Nagai, unable to cope up with the violent crowd stood aside to beg a small piece of meat. She lost in the race to food as nobody cared about her moaning. The people pouncing upon the prey fiercely sliced down all the meat leaving a mere skeleton. The vultures, crows and dogs gathered themselves for their share of food too but ended up on the losing side in the battle against men.

Nilya, unable to battle his share out stood afar. He tried to push through the crowd but was thrown back lacking the strength among those fierce men. Kisnya, being slightly compassionate towards Nilya threw a few chunks of solid meat at him. His troughs were overflowing with meat. Here the author metaphorically portrays the pathetic imbalance and lack of equality in our society. Kisnya threw the pieces of meat not only with compassion but also with humiliation.

After the celebration of animalistic battle was over the people returned covered in blood. Every part of their body was reddened with blood. The blood here is highly metaphorical as the author intends to portray the horrible casualty of the war going on between men and men. It doesn't take a weapon to shade blood. We're all covered with the blood of those people whose wretchedness, oppression and death we are responsible for.

After the people left with their shares Nilya tried to find the traces of meat layered on the remaining bones to fill his pot. He then had to battle with the vultures and dogs. He could finally manage to have some meat to satisfy his family but it was just the prelude. When he started moving towards home the vultures and crows tailed him to have their share of meal. Nilya started running with unsteady steps and ended up falling in a bush. His leg was wounded by the thorn-pricks. The dogs came over to take away the bones as his pot fell down. He, in order to save himself and his family from starvation tried to retrieve the pieces covered in dust.

The story comes to an abrupt end here as Nilya continues to heap the bones into his pot and the vultures hover over his head as a symbol of the society that has pushed the Mahars into this life of wretchedness. The buzzards are those who have snatched the rights from the oppressed.

Keshav Meshram's *Barriers*

The civilisation knew no discrimination until personal agendas overwhelmed the sense of social welfare. The civilised society created barriers with religion, with culture and belief and even with the pigmentation of skin. A sector of people seeking power and possession demeaned and diminished others by putting on barricades. The Hindu society, to be more specific the Bramhinist community put on the barricade by the means of communal discrimination. The people who were low on their proclaimed hierarchy were deprived of social rights, education and dignity. They had been termed as 'Achchut' as the Bramhinist community treated them as untouchables and it's truly humiliating if a fellow human being detests the touch of another human being. The treatment carried on for centuries and still carries on even in present time. The world has moved forward but the narrow despicable practices still thrive on. The discrimination received a flurry of protests from human right activists and many more. After 1956 the Dalits in Maharashtra and Uttarpradesh started converting themselves into Buddhists. But that didn't change the mentality of Bramhins and other upper castes towards them. The Bramhinists always wanted to dominate the Mahars, Mangs and other communities in order to solidify their dominance and superiority over them. Their progress was prohibited by the impasse created by the system. Humanitarians raised their voice but couldn't uproot the prejudice that had mingled itself with marrows.

The story is of being deprived, demeaned and finally motivated to raise some defiance against the stale system. Keshav Meshram creates hope in his short story the 'Barriers' and enkindles a pyre that will turn into a devastating flame to devour the society. Zingu and his son Narayan come to Murtijapur for Narayan's further education. Zingu is a man humbled by his occupation and his masters who has dreams gleaming in his eyes – dreams to educate his son Narayan and rid him from the accursed chain of their enslaving profession. He works under Deshmukh family who are seemingly comparatively nice to his family. Though Deshmukh was vehemently against the idea of Narayan's going to hostel to have independent education Zingu was steady at his decision. He insisted on Narayan's liberty and finally was able to set him free from the stalemate position they lived in.

Though Zingu had taken a bold step towards seeking liberty for his son his behavior in the roads of Murtijapur was depicting sharply his dominated soul all over as he was greeting everyone with a bough. When Narayan answered a Bramhin at being asked his name Zingu palpitated because of his complex about his caste. Though the mass conversion at Dadhi-Pedhi had already occurred there was no change in the viewpoints of Feudal lords and other upper-caste people. They backed down at the ferocity and scale of the movement but raised back up to dominate the oppressed as they used to do. The table was about to turn but the diminishing eyes of the Bramhinists remained the same. Idols of Hindu Gods were forsaken but the awe still remained in the dominated minds of the Dalits. People like Deshmukh were not yet ready to spare them the equal rights.

Narayan and Zingu reached the home of headmaster Dongre where they were welcomed after Dongre received the letter from Deshmukh. Zingu was literally knelt to him all the time as he told Narayan time and again that 'Guru' was next to God only. His enslaving gestures were to prove his obedience and submission to the 'authority' as it was for the sake of his son's future.

Narayan was a well-built boy having a more advanced physique compared to most boys of his age. Unlike his father his character shows no signs of that fragility or trembling as he knew his position and maintained and uplifted it. He's more of a calm and steady boy with a silent flame inside his heart. He was initially welcomed by the headmaster and the school also and made some friends too. He was earning rewards for his athletic prowess and other activities. But the things began to change when he came late in the school at the day when he went to receive Raghaba Kamble from station. Raghaba Kamble was the head of the Backward Castes Association of Akola district. He was a rebellious figure amongst the oppressed students and teachers too. He tried to uplift the position of Dalit students by explaining to the Buddhism and humanitarianism. He tried to make the education system a better place for the oppressed students.

After being late at school Narayan had to face the punishment of the headmaster and he was maintaining his obedience until things started to twist into another direction. His punishments turned out to be more painful and sickening as he was compelled to serve at headmaster's home. He had to cut woods or do other hectic jobs. He was deprived from the district sports meet and had to face the fury of the headmaster every single day. It was the headmaster who was determined to push him down and dishearten him at any cost. After Narayan spoke to Raghaba the fury turned into a tormented rage unable to explode. Narayan drew something on his notebook in the class which didn't please the headmaster at all. The headmaster was made to eat jalebi from Narayan's hand and definitely it was something to hammer on the prejudice of the headmaster. As a form of revenge, he was sent to a tribal settlement to fetch 'medicine' for Vatsalabai. He did the job with no big sweat. Narayan was already dejected with the headmaster. And, their mentality towards Narayan came to clarity when his friend. Sampat's father treated his presence repulsively. And afterwards it struck Narayan with full velocity when he heard his headmaster blabbering abuses towards him while intoxicated. The venality and hypocrisy of the headmaster was clear to him with his observations and the unauthorised relationship between the headmaster and Vatsalabai. The flame was turning into the blast since Narayan left for attending Anusuya's engagement who was Raghabadada's niece.

The defiance of Narayan has been portrayed at the climax of the story. Dressed in a dhoti and turban he entered headmaster's house and set a pile of wood on fire as a symbol of his vehement protest against the oppression he had to face. The burst of flames not only signified his raising defiance but also created the beginning of a larger fire of resurrection.

Anna Bhau Sathe's *Gold from the Grave*

Marathi Dalit literature produces some of the most chilling pictures of society which are as real as blisters and are drenched in dark anguish. Anna Bhau Sathe pulls out from his arsenal a horrific portrait of darkness; darkness that is produced by the burning flame of hunger inside the stomach of thousands of Dalits. Well, if we leave the Dalit scenario behind before going through the story it will still be standing as a reflection of the wretched livelihood in the remote villages in this country. There are several shades of human psyche portrayed distinctly in this story. On one hand, there is a vehement justification for every bit of war against hunger and then there is lust on the other hand. Lust that beholds the frivolity of capitalist society is just another form of need.

The story portrays kind of a metamorphosis where a low earning man driven by his hunger and responsibilities turns into a ghoulish mammonite. Bheema, the protagonist in the story plays a negative character in the story. But, there lays something underneath all the darkness. All the characters in the story, including the jackals have their own justified perspectives behind their respective actions.

Bheema in the story is a well-built man with an impressive physique and physical prowess. On the very first note he appears to be a brave countryman with a passionate urge to feed his family. His harsh and bold outlook is very uneven in match with his fatherly amour for his daughter. There is a certain indication of his lack of affinity towards urban life or to be more specific the life of Bombay. After his failed attempts in the city he found his refuge finally in the jungle where he found a job as a stone quarry worker. But as they say "nothing lasts forever". The flamboyant rock-crusher's dreams came crashing down when his contract was over. A man's worst nightmare is to watch his wife and child burn in starvation and poverty. Chills ran down his spine as his dreary thoughts create the emaciated faces of his wife and daughter. At that dire moment 'death' appeared in front of him as the last floating straw and showed him a glimpse of hope. He found his new source to earn his living amidst the ashes and remains of a funeral pyre.

It is not much of an unusual case. According to the religious practices some of the valuable adornments are left with the dead leading to their funeral. In the village areas people still cremate the dead in 'Chitah'. So, the poor undertakers would snatch the valuables from the corpse. Bheema took this work as his new profession and it was fairly profitable and moreover it was not harming anybody literally. And, with this ghoulishly noble profession a humanist perception grew in his mind. According to Bheema, the poor shouldn't deserve to die because of the rich. The jobless rich men were the ones he wanted to be dead. The rich often adorn the corpse of their near ones with gold. Not only funeral pyres, Bheema invaded the graves too. With a macabre blooming inside Bheema seemingly succeeded to feed his family. So, this was all approved by his conscience and justified to his ideology.

Soon the whole thing drew attention as the graves were found dug and corpses taken out. Bheema's wife wasn't very fond of her husband's business and it was evident from her words. But Bheema stood firm with his justification as this was the only way visible to him to feed his family and fulfil their wills. He was stuck between bravery and slavery. He certainly had a noble cause if we assess his practices as just another way of earning livelihood. But the essence and tone was really dark and ghoulish. It was detestable as an act. And, when his priorities were fulfilled he went on to conceive the lust of gold. He certainly wished more of luxury for his family.

Just like hunger lust has its own violent abyss and Bheema was wallowing into the depth of his own darkness. His Dionysian morality drove him towards a mammonish craving. His resolutions are backed up by the lines: "The city of Bombay itself is a colony of ghosts. The real spectres live in the houses and the dead one's rot in the grave." Bheema here talks from his bitter experience in the city. 'The ghosts' are definitely metaphorical here just like Dracula is a metaphor representing the bourgeois. Bheema's introspection is based on hard realism.

He then leaves for that night's work as his morbid psyche content with the news of that rich man's death. Here the narrator creates a dark ambience for the finalising of his ghoulish character. When he left, he had already turned into that mammonite completely. The climax of his transformation is also accompanied by that same audacity of his and of course another figure to take his position in the cycle. That figure turned out to be a pack of jackals who were lured by the odor of the corpse Bheema dug out of the grave. Then a vicious battle between man and beast takes place in the graveyard. Bheema's lust and strength was victorious against the hunger and claws of the jackals. But, somewhere in the battle Bheema seemed more like the tyrant community and the jackals the oppressed and dominated.

The jackals created wounds on the muscular body of Bheema but the real cost he had to pay was in the hands of the corpse. With the roars and groans the villagers were alerted and went searching the graveyard. In his lust and haste Bheema's hand was trapped inside the jaw of the corpse in which rigor mortis set in. He succeeded in freeing his but at the cost of his fingers. His preference was switched to his crave to escape alive. Bheema's story here comes to a cathartic end when he learns that the quarry work would start again. With his fingers his pride, lust and audacity were amputated too at the end of the story.

Avinash Dolas's *The Refugee*

Before analysing the story if we look at the title it claims to be equivalent to 'homeless' and 'home' has numerous definitions. 'Home' can be judged as the residence within four walls or something beyond that physical structure. If we judge the word from a metaphysical point of view it may refer to a territory, a community, a country or race. In one way or another there are lots of people who have lost their refuges despite living in their own homes. And, on another hand there are people banished or lost from their home, their country. Like in today's world thousands of people in countries like Kuwait and Syria have turned into refugees due to the vicious war going on. Their homes are perhaps turned to dust due to *Explosions* or maybe they have been driven out by the invading forces from their residences. The story 'The Refugee' was written at the times of wretchedness when there was a war going on in Bangladesh and thousands of Hindus were forced to immigrate. They had to leave their country and settle down in India for good with literally nothing in hand. The story revolves around the narrator's inert monologue and well concludes the short story section of the book by Dangle. Avinash Dolas, the author, brings out the heavy spree of emotions that brew and explode in the conscious of a Dalit in India. The abandonment is highly metaphorical. The story begins with his banishment at the age of twenty-one from his village. Some kind of altercation had transpired between him and the influential ones in the village that would later be disclosed at the end of the story. The story receives a sudden beginning where the young protagonist turns into a refugee.

His mother pleads to him to leave the village with a heart-breaking urgency. It's literally unbelievable that a mother would perform this kind of disowning to her son. But it was the circumstances that compelled her to react the way she did. The protagonist was the one who raised the voice and stood up against the upper castes in the village when they tried to force the Mahars to empty a well. Before that they beat a Mahar woman at her drinking from that well which belonged to a high-caste. The whole village beat up the Mahars like beasts and deprived them from food and water. He fired the artilleries that had been stacking up inside his head for twenty-one years. He had faced twenty-one years of domination, racism, wretchedness and more distinctively humiliation. His voice spoke for the millions of voiceless Dalits all over India. And, he had to pay the cost for his defiance. There isn't an authority in this world that's deliberate towards anarchy. He was threatened to ask for forgiveness, grovel and prostrate before the dominants. Otherwise his house with his family would be burned. Under this dire consequence his mother pleaded him to leave the village for good.

The protagonist was a righteous man. There are two kinds of oppressed people in this world: one, who get beaten, smitten and humiliated and still without a sharp word against the authority consider their wretchedness as their piteous destiny; and the other, who in return to their humiliation send back a repulsive strike at the authority. The protagonist belonged to that second category. But he was young and without his family, vulnerable. He was a posthumous child and his rebellious protest was killed before it could lead to any change. The thought that his mother had disowned him saddened him the most. He was turned into an orphan within seconds and didn't belong to his people anymore. Hiding his grief, he left the village and his emotions groped him with the sense of parting. He tried to console himself with philosophies but his pain – his rage – his fury stung him again and again. There was nothing but the road burning under his feet, the merciless sun, a sweat-soaked handkerchief and his memories of wretchedness. His chappals gave up but his feet didn't, just like his forebears who had never stepped up against the slimy customs and tenuous folds of casteism, racial discrimination but he did. He, in his soliloquy stated: "My name itself is a curse." His statement wasn't just a lament from a man of despair. It was something very evident on the very scenario where the lower castes were treated as detestable animals and the humiliation came only because of their surnames. It's still a heinous custom that carries on its vendetta.

The crowding thoughts inside his head made him fatigued as he finally reached the station. Rapid rush of emotions in his head were described efficiently with stabbing statements in his soliloquy. He had nowhere to go and it meant he could go anywhere, wherever the road would carry his feet to. There was the world running on with Santu's life staggered in a station crowded with strangers. He observed a beggar trying to gulp rough pieces of bread with noisy bites as if the whole oppressed community was trying to gulp down the morsels thrown to them. He went back in his memory lane as he observed the people around him. Chandra who used to sell her body to a grocer under the grim claw of poverty once asked him to lend her five rupees to take her son to the doctor. Her husband was bed-ridden as he lost his limbs in an *Explosion*. He refused to lend her money, in fact, he couldn't. He felt a wave of revulsion in his body when he saw a man eating with fingers which were wasted, broken and with oozing pus and blood. The vicious ugliness of the world unveiled itself before him.

His rebellious blood boiled up when the train arrived and a water carrier served water to a woman in a compartment and her husband poured down the water to solidify the same disdainful casteism. He wished to run down and throttle all the people he had met including himself as his repulsion and dejection had reached the climax. The hatred between men and men, the distress and the baseless disdain were turning him into a misanthrope.

When he entered the compartment, he met some people who were just like him, homeless. There was a man named Surji who had come from Bangladesh as there was massacre going on. He came to India to find refuge at his relative's place in Mumbai. He was a refugee from his country. He had to immigrate to India living everything behind that once belonged to him. Just because of the hatred between men Surji had lost his home. India, the country that provided thousands of Bangladeshis with shelter has refugees of its own who live in the country itself. The massacre found its victims in the Hindus, no matter upper-caste or lower. And, people like Shantu had been the victim of the same hatred, only in another form and it snatched their home away. They, although living in the same country, were discriminated, cornered. The country that gives refuge to the homeless cannot make itself a 'home' for some people. Santu were Surji were standing at the same crossroad but there was an ironic contrast. Surji was finding his home in an entirely new country but he had a relative in there. And, Santu was homeless in his own homeland devoid of a single face to call his own. The oppressed, they are still homeless in their own country.

3

Survival and Other Stories: Bangla Dalit Fiction in Translation

Gobindo Shoundo's story *Jale Dangai* (Tr. *On Water and on Shore*)

On Water and on Shore is the translation of the 1996 Bengali story, by Gobindo Shoundo, *Jale Dangai* published in Chaturtha Duniyar Galpo, which has depicted the hostilities and life risks of a fisherman, Shashi. All through the story the readers are able to see how toilsome it is to catch fish from the sea as it is able to snatch one's precious life. Shashi is a person who has learnt many things whom sea has taught many things but snatched away near and dear ones from him. But apart from that the story has exposed the very contrast between the water and the shore, as it becomes clear from the title of the story, Shashi remains in his poor territory in spite of all his hardships while Nagenbabu climbs up at the pinnacle of riches using his money. The story brings tears and thoughts on *dalit* exploitation in the consciousness of the readers. It has a very wonderful narrative technique to depict the miserable plight of the life of Shashi. The story has a strong comment on *Dalit* Consciousness that follows the footsteps of the fisherman Shashi.

In the very introduction part, the critics have spoken out on the story by Gobinda Shoundo,

> "Gobinda Shoundo's story *Jale Dangai* (*On Water and on Shore*) is a sad tale of a poor fisherman, Shashi who gets struck in a tempest during his routine trip to the sea in search of fish.

The power relation in the rungs of society is so heavily one sided that the mainstream myth of progress seems a distant dream to this hapless social marginals."

The story speaks of the hostile life of the persons who constantly fight with death to earn their livelihood. The story has mentioned the death of the elder son of Shashi, who faced his doom in a tempest at the sea. For a father, it is unimaginable to feel how grief it evokes to see the death of his own son in front of his eyes.

In spite of these grievous incidents, Shashi constantly struggles for his existence. The people like Nagen Sharma who are, the real demons of the shore are the people who deceive the poor men to execute their purpose. The story shows how Nagenbabu, takes all the profit of Shashi, by creating a bizarre story of the rotten fishes in midst of the story. Shashi understands Nagen's intention and fraud stories at the very end.

"Is God yours alone? Deep down, Shashi was seething with anger. So you lost all you had and still the bank gave you all this money? A lie! The fish turning bad, your weeping all these were cock and bull stories."

But he fails to protest and ends up the conversation with Nagen Sharma by a meagre *Hmm.* This expresses evidently the *dalit* numbness in front of their money lenders. Where Shashi is completely helpless, his consolation is only three thousand rupees that Sharma gave to him. Thus, the story serves as a very important element in *Dalit* literature.

Makhanlal Pradhan's *Gopal Chashir Jat Dharma* (Tr. *Farmer Gopal's Caste and Creed)*

The story *Farmer Gopal's Caste and Creed* is the translation of the 1996 story, *Gopal Chashir Jatdharma,* published in Chaturtha Duniayar Galpo, that speaks of a person who is compelled to change his job time and again with caste heading towards and uncertain future. He finds himself being intimidated into giving up his productive land and traditional occupation of agriculture to suti the needs of the rapacious land mafia who wished to change the face of Kolkata and after that he is forced to change deliberately his jobs and sometimes live his life as a coolie, then a mason and finally the readers are able to see that he is living a life no better than he lived in earlier days. And even worse while he is forced by government to give his pond up to them and be a fisherman Gopal Ghosh fights against all these whimsicalities of the society and superiors who always dominate over them to serve their own purpose and when the job is done, never even care about their welfare and refuses to give the pond to government. The entire story shows a glance of Gopal's hope in adolescence to be a citizen of a giant city. His uncertainty in various jobs, his vast alteration of jobs after jobs that has enabled him to practice among all caste and religion basically among Muslims and his lost hopes. The story shows that in a *dalit*'s society like the persons, who follow the footsteps of Gopal Gosh, there is no territory of religion or caste, the only thing that matters is the unprivileged people are forced to live in one society, the society of marginalised people. Gopal has proved himself to be a member of a society where there is no caste or religion but only the immense scarcity of money. The narrator has gifted the readers the very important thoughts on their state or rather the life at stake which has a strong impre3ssion over *dalit* consciousness. In the introduction part, the critics have commented on the story,

> "Makhanlal Pradhan's Gopal Chashir Jatdharma (Farmer Gopal's Caste and Creed) is a moving tale of a *dalit* farmer who has to try his luck in different professions in search of his livelihood."

The very character of Gopal Ghosh has been portrayed with unique virulence and unique perfection. He and his father fail victim to the erroneous hopes of becoming a city dweller as his father, Kedar's illiteracy and extreme innocence led them to lose their lands of farming to the government one way (as convinced by some people Kedar went to the office to put his signature.) But the dreams never came true. This incident has displayed a very common phenomena of our society, i.e. the miserable plight of the marginalised people and how rapid *dalit*isation takes place on basis of economic stability. It is to be taken critically that the government has no concern for them but for their lands and its conveyance. At every step of his life Gopal has seen that actually nobody is caring for them. He had to change his job again and again for supporting him and his family. In course of his alteration of jobs he became a masin which is regarded by a number of people in the society, a work of Muslims. At this point, Gopal makes a comment that exposes the secular mindset of the hungry ones.

"Do the poor have any caste identity? Who is going to offer me the job of a Hindu? You give me one." this statement of Gopal evidently exposes, he is not farmer anymore, in fact, he has been intermingled with several religions and castes that has at last left an impression in him i.e. he has only one caste, one religion, it is hunger and poverty.

Atlast, he gets agitated from constant negligence and refuses to give his pond to the government as being a revolt against the dominant attitude of the rich ones. The story turns out some of the royal pictures of our country, somewhat ironical. India, with its constant *dalit*isation and a long barrier between the rich and poor ones can never be the greatest. No matter how loud the cry of the son of the Mukherjee family is.

"India will again be the greatest of the world's nations"

Gopal's near and dear one try to convince him by such words,

"Do the poor have any God? For the poor work is the only thing which matters."

That indicates rampant *dalit*isation of have-nots have somehow one way or the other succeeded to diminish the caste related or racial ego among the *dalit*s themselves. It seems, at the end of the story, that India has divided itself into two parts, the rich ones who dominate and the poor ones who are deliberately forced to accept their miserable plight for filling the hungry stomach.

Kapil Krishna Thakur's *Anya Ihudi* (*The Other Jew*)

The Other Jew is the translation of the 1996 Bengali Story, *Anya Ihudi* by Kapil Krishna Thakur published in Chaturtha Duniyar Galpo that tales of a burning ache of helplessness of a number of persons in both their motherland and neighbouring country who become a subject of hatred and deprivation at every sphere of life. The story gives space to Bishtu Pandit, once recognised in his own land as a teacher and therefore a man of social importance has been forced to escape from his homeland in the turbulent period of 71. A different kind of *dalit*isation that traumatises the innocent lives gets celebrated in both East Pakistan and India. The narrator has vehemently presented the character of Bishtucharan, with the intermingling of his face as a teacher and his face as a father. He constantly tries out to find,

> "O Bejo, my Bejo for what then did you leave your home behind? What is your real home?"

all through the story. This story is able to open our eyes towards a particular portion of time locked in history and rampant *dalit*isation of persons based on religion and residence that takes place even today also at various segments of contemporary society.

In the introduction part the critics have stated about the story,

> "Kapil Krishna Thakur's Anya Ihudi (The Other Jew) manifests the helplessness of a large number of refugee Bengali families who were driven out of erstwhile East Pakistan during and after partition."

All through the story, lies shadows of shame, deprivation, injustice, extreme level of anguish, sorrow, religious animosity and most of all, political; indifference towards a particular crowd of men. The protagonist Bishtucharan, a former teacher of a village school in East Pakistan stays on even after the partition showing no immense power of patriotic love. However, he is compelled to uproot his family from the ground of Bangladesh due to tragic circumstances of the gang-rape and death of Jhumu, his daughter.

> "that dirty, rotten scoundrel Ferumiya. One day when Jhunu was coming back from college, Feru and his mates kidnapped her. Feru wanted to marry her. She did not agree. They assaulted her all through the night and just before daybreak…"

Unwanted occurrences fell on Bistucharan like a thunder. This incident shows how religion has created a barrier of mishaps in his life. Ferumiya took the advantage of Jhunu being a Hindu and mercilessly raped her. The suffering of Bisthu in Bangladesh in this turbulent time shows how rapid *dalit*isation based on religion alienated the minor Hindus, making them extremely trivial on society so that they get compelled to leave their home and head towards India.

Fearing the same fate for his younger daughter Rhunu, he comes to stay with Brajabasi, a former friend and relative who fled in India. In India they are forced to live beside the train lines. The society and the giant politicians have deserted them of all opportunities and advantages. Not only that they are rather regarded as "Banglu" (refugees) by the people. Still they cherish a hope of a better life even knowing it is not possible. Within a night, it seems a crowd of people living in Bangladesh lost their identity as well as unique existence in society and were marginalised based on religious dogmas. Situation turned more grievous when one day Rhunu, Cheno, her cousin and several other girls of their colony are seized and gangraped by the goons of the local leaders. Bishtucharan's pathetic fate somehow ignites the fire of anger within him and it comes out in the form of bewilderment and tears and his hitting himself.

All the story depicts how a crowd of people is getting wounded in terms of minority that shows the very fact that it can be either caste or religion or financial power or something else but the consequence all the process of constant banishment and marginal people makes is nothing but the addition of a number of *dalit*s. Bishtucharan's life becomes an example of a number of people who later realised in the turbulent socio economical bias that they are not safe either in Bangladesh or in India. The partition, which comes out has become a milestone in the history of Bengal to engender a crowd of voiceless people who lived as a redundant section with no individual entity.

Goutam Ali's *Haat* (*Market Place*, translated as *Bazaar*)

Bazaar, a story translated by Jayjit Ghosh is a 1996 Bengali story *Haat* by Gautam Ali, published in Chaturtha Dunuyar Galpo. Though there is a little bit of difference between two terms Haat and Bazaar as to be sure the former term is more humble and native and appealing as well as fits appropriate with the central theme of the story but translated complementary Bazaar can also be marked as somewhat appropriate as it evokes the satirical state of the so called contemporary society. According to the glossary, a "haat" is a village market where goods are bought and sold. It is now evident to all of its readers that the name of the story itself has a strong impression on the commoditisation of women. On the surface, it is a tear evoking tale of two women but layers of meanings lie concealed within the story. One is the employer and the latter is the employee, the former is forced to accept the somewhat immoral and excessive sexual urge and sexual exploitation by her husband who being the money giver imposes all his sexual hunger as well as gratifies his lust from the latter who is an innocent poor village girl and is forced to

> "Submit to the libidinal demands of her middle aged upper class employer."

The story has received strong reactions from all kinds of critics the state of woman in our society has been highly emphasised throughout the story. A woman's several attempts to hold their own position in a society and as a means of it, the victimisation of several poor woman in the hands of a husband's lascivious nature forms the very eye catching realistic outlook towards a rotten society where woman are nothing but benumbed creatures. From the eye of the *dalit* critic, the story is,

> "a story of psycho-sexual urges and impulses."

It shows now the poor woman who came to a big city with a hope of "square meal and a settled state of living" have no individual entity and a subject to regular and often quiet, normal sexual molestation and still are forced to remain dumb in front of all sexual oppressions.

The story enlightens a very common portrayal of the modern society with its natural phenomena of the supremacy of the haves over have-nots. The mistress of the house and her husband represent the class where money speaks of power and power speaks of lust. However, in spite of having all the earthly pleasures and commodities they were deprived of the happiness of having a child. Nevertheless, they lived happily and the story takes a critical turn when,

> "The ebb and flow of life one day confined the woman to bed as she fell victim to gout."

At that time the woman started to look for the maid servants as a household help. All would have gone well unless the salacious nature of her husband has caused a number of mishaps in the family.

The incontinent character of her husband presents himself naked when he discovers that,

> "his wife had a lot to do apart from cooking. He must help her out."

Here the author has presented the husband's abnormal kind of sexual needs from the maid servant. As he is positioned at a supreme class in the society, as he is rich, he can buy his sexual ailments from an innocent girl and accept her as nothing but a means of gratifying his diabolic lust, the very thought has been highly exuberated throughout the story, his uncultured utterance,

> "This maid has awakened my sleeping lust"

Evidently expresses his psychological insight that has a clear and transparent reflection of the underlying malodour of the sexual exploitation of the voiceless section of the society of the *dalit*s.

The mistress ruthlessly and somewhat helplessly dismissed the maidservant as of suspecting her as the real culprit who influenced him to do such a thing. All these show how a maidservant is being humiliated without any vice being accused by not just a person but by an entire portion of the society.

However, the commoditisation as well as *dalit*isation of the woman can be seen distinctly in a particular part of the story where the husband returning home late speaks of a specific bazaar or rather a haat.,

> "Where did you go?" the wife was curious to know. She was applying lime on betel leaves.
>
> "I went to the haat"
>
> "You mean the haat of our town. "
>
> "I heard of it often. It was a crowded spectacle. It functions every day. But they sale only one commodity – dolls."
>
> "Dolls? You surprise me, what kind of doll? Her curiosity was un quenchable."
>
> "Yes – it's a doll. Alright! But it's not made of clay or plastic. It's of flesh and blood."

It should be taken critically how mercilessly the man symbolises the prostitute at the haat as "dolls." Well, dolls have no custom entity, they act according to their owners beckoning. Her husband also says without any sense of shame, the very statement which proves their commoditisation,

> "She is yours till there's money in your pocket."

Thus this symbol barely exposes the fact that how the large crowd belonging to the lower class dolls of "flesh and blood" are forced to act acquiescent to their superiors in spite of all the humiliations they face. They have no soul, no organs, only a bare structure is the possession of them. They are accustomed to act on their superior's wish. This very social practice has been turned out time and again in the story. The mistress just wants to hold her family with all her power. She makes desperate attempts to save her husband from being a subject of insult from her society. That is why, she exchanges a number of servants in the house. The father less girl of the village who came with a dream of a square meal and a settled state of living was handed over to the mistress of the house as a servant considering their affluence. The author himself states somewhat satirically,

> "it was an affluent household and there was nothing to worry about."

As if affluence and riches itself engenders courtesy but the real scenario became absolutely ironical to the statement. The girl leaves to her mother being a victim of her master's abusive lust.

At the very last paragraph the author again gives a stinging attack when he speaks humbly, "While reading Saratchandra one fine morning the woman again complained to her colleague about her gout. She must have a chirping chick – a maid young and buxom."

The very writer, who spoke of the *dalit*s, of the subalterns the people with the smell of mud, the people with the odour of sweat, can't even leave an impression on an educated woman living in a high class society. Here throughout the story, not a few women but an entire segment of a society has been victimised in the sinister hands of their superiors.

The story gives rise to a number of questions:

1. Is really money an answer of all abusive deeds?
2. Why the woman, especially the poor women are being victimised in the hands of the powerful?
3. Why are dream of a square meal turning into a nightmare?

Society remains mute while confronting these questions. There is no answer to it rather the husband's attitude towards the women of the lower class the mistresses several attempts to conceal her helplessness and the author's satirical statements gives a slap in the face of reality, in the face of the society gone wrong, with its false conventions.

Shyamal Kumar Pramanik's *Ekhono Adim* (Tr. *Survival*)

Survival, is the translation of 1996 story by Shayamal Kumar Pramanik, *Ekhono Adim* published in Chaturthya Duniyar Galpo. Though, the translated title of the story *Ekhono Adim* is entirely different from its original one but the title shows an eye-burning reflection of the situation of a person or rather the persons with a hungry stomach. The wise men all are the world have said indeed that man is a rational animal but de facto that very quality "rationality" is attributed to the well fed, well bred, well lived men only, whenever men are deprived of their basic needs, that very word, "rational" erases itself automatically, or to be true even, unknowingly. The story points out a situation just like this where a family is bereft of one of its basic desires, the food, and living a life no better than a brute. So, how can they abide by the rules of the very rationality? The name of the story, *Survival* has spoken a lot about its content. Whenever men are dying of hunger they can do, anything, even risking their lives just to bring in even a little bit of grain, Raju, the protagonist of the story, risks his life by fighting with a ferocious snake to get food. The story however shows the light of hope at the far end where Raju finally banishes the snake and finds grain for himself and for the rest of the family proving the appropriateness of the title. A man goes that far to snatch grain from a rat-hole. This shows the terrible condition of a man, helpless and at the same time to a primitive age in a modern era where situation, time and society makes a man a beast who can never know one day he was a rational animal.

The story has a strong comment on hunger. In the introduction, it is said,

> "Such gripping takes proudly proclaim the invincibility of *dalit* consciousness as reflected on literature."

The protagonist Raju Rajawan as well as his wife Matia and Sonu here is hungry for a lot of time. The very condition awakens the beast within him; he goes on searching the rat holes for a little grain of food. That the rat has taken. This situation somehow brings tears in the eyes of the readers. However, as the story goes we can see, the kind of life Raju have led throughout his life? His journey of life without destination indicates a crowd of people like Raju, who have no other hope but just something to eat. The name of his wife Matia, is also very significant as it shows a person born of soil, is bound to collect his or her ailments from the soil and perhaps end up in mingling up with it. To follow the glossary,

> "Matia: literally one born of the soil shows close connection between under privileged people and nature."

Matia is the embodiment of such persons who are afraid of fate even in an extreme hostile condition. It becomes evident in her statements;

> "Are you crazy? Do you want to kill it? Beware the snake Goddess."

But perhaps Gods and Goddesses pop up in the consciousness of a person till his stomach is full. Raju desperately inserts his hand into the rat hole to get some food. But to the reader's surprise the story has a happy ending as Raju finally collects food from that hole, banishing the snake but this little story speaks of our heart with its constant beatings of our reality with its unblinking glace on sufferings. Raju's father came to West Bengal with a hope.

> "The soils of Bengal are golden, nobody starves there."

without knowing that golden soils are unavailable in the world of an underprivileged man and starvation has become now a must for him who lives in the ground. However, this hope seems highly ironical when we see the real scenario, the terrible condition of this man constantly fighting against his life to get life in the guile of food. In several passages of the story, we are able to see not only he but also his wife and his little child has seen hunger as a constant threat of their lives. Time and society here play the role of a silent killer to them as the epitome of death. Raju, though living a scattered life never loses his hope throughout the end. The author wants to show that not some meagre glances, not some momentary tears, but a helping hand full of food us necessary to bring them back to human society. The reader gets a close vision of the life of this people who need empathy more than sympathy. The author shows how struggle becomes evident and a must to a person to survive though they don't deserve the life of a beast. This at the end, the reader follows the footsteps of Raju and sees nothing but the heart beatings of fear behind the apparent desperate attitude, underlying intense deprivation and tears of pain below the apparent inhuman attitude and above all, at the end, the uncertainty of tomorrow shadowed by the happiness and joy of today.

Manoranjan Barman's *Shabori*

Shabori is Bengali story by Manoranjan Barman, that has two protagonists, Rekaha and Padma, with the former representing the woman from a city suffering in a remote village while the latter, a woman of low caste, forced to give into the hands of the rogue. The word *Shabori* literally means a huntress. But here in this story the word has a unique existence that differentiates it from taking the word too literally. The title seems to portray an anguished sore face of a woman socially recognised as an incarnation of a low born forced to capitulate herself in the hands of nefarious lust that appears in the guile of Ratan Shashaml. On one hand there is Rekha who faces a sudden and accidental jeopardy as an outcome of her husband's (the narrator's) unanticipated unemployment as a result of losing his job in a private company which seems to reduce all her hopes to give her son Raju a better future possible only in a large city like Kolkata. On the other the author speaks of Padma, the shabori who is forced to keep physical relation with Shashmal babu, who killed both his father and husband. The author shows his mastery by showing two viewpoints as well as deciphering the real facts with proper historical evidence. This is a story, a fiction, intermingled with reality. The story shows at last, the utter helplessness of Padma who is unable to ignite the light of revolt as she has no other way-out. The story with its subtle psychological insight, into the characters, loyal descriptions, and showing common mass becoming victims of political agitations usage of proper words, real life incidents, the daily lives, with proper notice towards the rituals adds up spices to its delineation.

In the introduction part, the critics have said about the story,

> "Manoranjan Barman's "Shabori" (literally, huntress, here referring to a woman belonging to the lowly Shabor caste) highlights the different standpoints of the two protagonists – Padma and Rekha"

This story uses a large thematic canvas to empathise two individuals, who, for their unfortunate time face utter helplessness in two different standpoints. On one hand, there is Rekha who is basically a woman from a big city like Kolkata, so gradually she can't cope up with the rural cultures and rituals. In the story, the protagonist has lost his job due to the fact that his company is going to make multi-storey buildings. As a consequence, his wife and son, Rekha and Raju had to move to their village. Rekha finds her life utter hostile in this new place. Her fate shows how helpless people like the narrator are becoming the subject of negligence to the authority. It becomes evident when he speaks,

> "Everybody takes care of themselves these days. The multi storey building would have been made by the nephew of one of the big leaders. And Mukherjee is going to get a flat."

Which shows not just the industrial authorities but also the politicians take advantage of the poor workers and at last when their purposes done, they take no time to throw them off like a garbage that serves as an example of rampant *dalit*isation in the towns.

On the other hand, the story speaks of Padma, a Shabori who represent a completely abandoned caste of Indian rural society. This very picture of a caste, forbidden to entire human civilisation and forced to live outside the society.

"I guess they were no mads at one point of time, before settling on state owned lands near the canal at the end of the village."

The humiliation over Shabors with a false notion that they are thieves from their very basic instincts gives a clear picture of the *dalit* humiliation in the rural areas.

"As a matter of fact, whenever there was a theft or any such crime, the police would pick some of the Shabor men for questioning irrespective of their guilt or in nonsense."

The story also points out, the victimisation of the *dalit*s, of the poor ones in the cruel hands of political turbulence and agitation. The death of Prananath Shabor, Padma's husband and Bholanath Dolui undoubtedly speaks of a number of deaths of a common mass who had to pay with their lives for their very common place demands.

"Padma's husband Prananath Shabor on our side and Bhogirath Dolui of the opposition died."

Moreover, the story gives a final attack to the readers when it aware us of the very fact of "booking Padma by Shashmal babu to fulfil his carnal lust. The fate of Padma brings tears to our eyes. She had to submit herself to Shashmal babu, who killed her husband. She has no way. The rapid humiliation over *dalit*s has snatched her words. The story provides a clear reflection of a bitter reality that can be expanded into a novel.

Achinta Biswas's *Bipralabdha* (Tr. *The Deceived*)

The Deceived is the translation of the 1996 Bengali story *Bipralabdha* by Achintya Biswas published in Chaturthya Duniyar Galpo that speaks the tension between a priest who sees competition in Gopal Thakur an outsider who pretends to be a sadhu, and low caste Maya, his companies in spiritual practices ends in revenge of the high-caste. The story is written in a spectacular style that bears a humble appeal to all the readers. At the centre of the story lies Monahar Sadhukhan, who, previously a thief later turned himself into spirituality. He was a man of spirituality apparently but lust was deeply lied inside his heart stealthily. Later he finds real taste of spirituality within when his beard is cut showing a sign of insult. On the other hand, there is Maya who acts as if the Goddess Mahamaya have spelled a cast over her, falls in love with Dhananjay and finally finds redemption in flying away with him. The story is long with wonderful sketches of public life, character sketches and rituals and beliefs. It has a large thematic canvas that can be easily extended into a fully-fledged novel. The story is laced with the shadow of caste discrimination and caste hierarchy as well as political bias.

In the introduction par, the critics have commented on the story,

> "*Bipralabdha* (*The Deceived*) by Achintya Biswas is a long story of immeasurable suffering in the life of two *dalit* individuals – Gopal and Maya."

The story ends up with an intense sense of grief that indicates a sense of humiliation over the *dalit*s. The so-called progressive intellectuals who proudly assert that the curse of untouchability has left West Bengal forever, should visit the arid regions of the western part of Bengal to get the real picture.

The hypocrisy of the political leaders and parties appears naked in front of the readers in these lines,

> "They raised the same slogan:' Workers of the world, unite.' But none of them allowed the Bauris to enter their homes."

Situation turns grievous when Golap, who being a *dalit* went to protest, only to lie for three months at Dendua hospital but the hospital refused to take his admission which caused his un timely death.

"They did not allow us to enter Rupnarayanpur and neither could we go to Mihijam' said someone from the crowd. The whole night they just left him unattended at Kulti hospital. In the first hour of the morning, Golap, the son of a Bauri, died, leaving a son and a young wife behind." "He had just wanted water."

This indicates how caste system prevails in the place rampantly. The horrendous utterance "son of a Bauri" by the author has become a somewhat sarcastic one as if this very attribute of him caused his death.

When Maya in the form of Mahamaya, tried to protest against it by speaking out that she will drink their blood, the two corrupt, high-caste person, Nilu and Anamay sent goons to the temple where Gopal and Maya resided and they cut the beard and matted hair of Gopal, trying to prove his futility of spirituality and what is more pathetic, brutally raped her (Maya). All these shows how caste discrimination walks on triumphantly over dead bodies of Golaps of our society.

Susnata Jana's *Mahashweta Gramer Mukunda Ebong Ek Ascharjo Pronoy* (*Mukunda and an Extraordinary Love Affair*)

Mukunda and an Extraordinary Love Affair is the translation of the 1996 Bengali story, *Mahasweta Gramer Mukunda Ebong Ek Ascharja Pranoy* published in Chaturtha Duniyar Galpo, that has used a completely different canvas to picture the heart-beatings of two lovers irrespective of their caste in a village where this evil practice of caste discrimination has been deeply rooted into the psyche of the villagers. The very Mahasweta Gram performs as a location where all the incidents of this story take place. The writer has evidently spoken of our heart and has found the definition of true education. The story however is full of Mukunda's thoughts and experiences. The story contains all that is needed to make a story truly spectacular in the eyes of the readers. The title has spoken of an "extraordinary" love affair which serves as the main and most interesting part of the story. Susnata Jana, the writer of the story has depicted a story that has touched our heart.

In the introduction, Critics have commented on the story,

> "Susnata Jana's story *Mahasweta Gramer Mukunda Ebong Ek Ascharja Pranoy* has captured the political space of change in a blood spectrum."

Mukunda here plays the role of as helpless farmer and at the same time he has to bear the burden of his caste, a fisherman that gives him much trouble. Though he is not a fisherman any more, he is still a subject of laughter to Ambar Bhattacharjee, the newly elected Panchayat leader,

> "Hey, fisherman's brat, how goes the family business?"

On the other hand, it becomes ironical, when this very person, Ambar Bhattacharjee, in his speech speaks against, racial discrimination and caste discrimination.

"Friends, I promise to turn Mahasweta into an ideal village where there will be no darkness, no class distinction. Bonds of love will hold the village together. It will be a village of our dreams, where there will be non-enmity between the high and the low."

However, the actual state of the village is completely an antitheist to the imaginary place, Ambarbabu is creating in his speech.

But in spite of all these occurrences Mukunda finds peace within himself when he sees, Raju, Ambarbabu's son has fallen in love with Amli, Mukunda's daughter. Raju, in this story shows what the real term "education" means. The writer somehow seems to indicate, a sense of optimism with the fact that the younger generation has gone far beyond the caste distinction and on the other hand love, knows only one caste and that is mankind. Thus, the story though having an uncertain and sudden end shows the light of hope and the death of caste distinction in the time to come.

"Mukunda wondered if whatever Ambar had been saying in his speech had come true after all."

Thus' at some point it seems, "Mahasweta" is not merely the name of a village in Bengal; it stands witness to the psychological transformation in the young representatives of the new generation upper-caste people who desire to transcend the barrier of "untouchability."

Sunil Kumar Das's *Dhani Bauri Ganga Pelo* (*Dhani Bauri Gets 'Salvation'*)

Dhani Bauri Gets 'Salvation' is the Bengali story *Dhani Bauri Ganga Pelo* by Sunil Kumar Das published in "Gram Ganjer Galpo" depicting a very loyal scenario of this country which speaks of equality in the true sense of the term but in vain, that gets reflected in several passages of the story turning the reader's heads to the raging problem of caste hierarchy. The story goes on delineating on a long period of time. And what is strikingly awesome, the story begins at the scene of fag end of it. That is, the ending part pops up in front of the eyes of the readers which make them enthusiastic to gather and to focus their consciousness to look into the picture of the whole story which takes a long time of almost 35 years to limn an entire picture of unconditional love, pretention, and deprivation. The very word "salvation" is identical to get Ganges as the holy river is believed to preserve and ornamented seat in heaven after someone's death in Hindu mythology. The title indirectly indicates that it is quite unnatural for the untouchable woman like Dhani Bauri to get salvation. The story is written in a conversational method of narration. Two speakers Subhas and Nilu, who appears as somewhat modern and neoteric in their ideology, gradually converse with each other, telling the entire story in a unique pattern that unknowingly reflects the caste discrimination and caste hierarchy even among the *dalit*s themselves. Dhani Bauri who unconditionally loved and became the mother of Hiru Majhi, who being a bit eminent in caste hierarchy, fails to be her son he shows a kind of sense of pity and relief after her death indicating her presence in the house as awkward occurrence taking place for a long time. His wife also scorns and insults Dhani Bauri from entering to their kitchen in spite of being a subaltern in caste. All their concern seems to be on her money. However, the story gives a long description of Dhani's life, which serves as a material to reveal the veil of the "great communists" like Hiru as well as to indicate the inhuman attitude a helpless woman gets all through her life being like an alien in his country.

In the introduction, the critics have delivered as few words on the story,

> "The story is quite unconventional in its attempt to portray the hierarchy among various *dalit* communities. Ironically, the greater *dalit*, a female employee in Coal India contributes her earning for the welfare of the "lesser" *dalit* family."

On the surface the story appears to be the biography of Dhani Bauri, of her early life, her marriage, her loneliness, her affection towards Hiru Maji, a number of insults as a result of it and at last Dhani's tragic death. The author at first, gives a faint light of hope, at the very beginning if the story, where Dhani is carried to Magra. It somehow seems to the reader, that her sin Hiru Maji takes so care of her that he is organising all things for her salvation. But as the story goes, we come across layers of sorrow and suffering, of deprivation and insult, concealed within the salvation. The narrator at the very first part of the story throws a very suitable question to the readers,

> "If mere utterance of 'hari bol' could purify the human body and mind, why do the untouchables remain in the same miserable condition year after year? Why don't they get social acceptance even when they spend the entire Baishakh month uttering 'hari bol.'"

This very question evidently arouses the concern of the narrator, Nilu for the *dalit*s as well as gives the reader a sharp blow on his psyche. It however serves as a sardonic prologue to the story that gives a grievous account of her life full of lugubrious tears.

All false rituals with their camouflaging pretentions appear to be naked on front of bitter reality. Dhani Bauri had loved Gopal Maji's son Hiru whole heartedly. Unfortunately, she was gifted with nothing except insult as a return the story has a strong reaction towards her miserable condition and it is inevitable that Gopal Maji's family had never conceived her as a member of their family, the very rotten concept of caste discrimination and hatred towards the "below-standard" people have been deeply rooted within their psyche. It is a very astonishing and annoying fact that ironically, to be true, Gopal Maji and his family are by caste, Farmers i.e., sudras too. But in spite of being a subaltern, they belong to a comparatively higher class than that of Dhani Bauri. So being as citizen of this country which indirectly indulges its citizens to *dalit*ise people as following caste hierarchy. They are bound to be a part of this caste discrimination. The attitude of Hiru after Dhani

Masi's sraddha ceremony, towards Subodh, the other narrator indicates his actual nature and gives or provides a repercussion of what he actually used to think about Dhani Bauri who in spite of nor conceiving him in her womb, loved him as a son. Ad this love knew no riches, condition and social barriers that society makers create to ensconce their own purpose.

Anil Gharai's *Punascha Parashuram* (*Tr. Reincarnation of Parashuram*)

Reincarnation of Parashuram is the translation of the 2010 Bengali story, *Punascha Parashuram* by Anil Gharai published in Kak O Ananya Galpo, that has presented the dire poverty and opaqueness of the dalits in veteran manners by using the allusion of the myth of Parashuram. At the centre of the story, stands Sunar and her Husband, Bhisnath Barlar bewildered by their child's acute sickness and high fever. Bhisnath refuses to take his child Madho to hospital for cure showing a lack of proper consciousness when his wife requests him to do it. There will be no remission of this fever in the hospital. He, even consults and takes help from local Gunins (a sort of witch doctor that shows his lack of any medical education indeed.) Mangala, who after failing to cure Madho refers Bhisnath's mother as a witch making Bhisnath to kill her mercilessly in order to save the life of his child. At last, the child dies and Bhishnath gets a realisation of his guilt and manages to pay the ransom of his guilt by killing Mangala. The story has a totally unique approach on *dalit* superstitions which opened a completely new window of subaltern literature. The author, Gharai has chosen a peerless theme and content to narrate that makes the readers eyes glued to the worlds from beginning to end. Specially, the revival of the myth of Parashuram into their story has added a special flavour to it. It can be well said that the story is extraordinary in approach, humble in choice of words and at the same time very appealing to its content.

The story brings out a completely different aspect of life of the *dalit*s. It shows, how after celebrating 70 years of independence *dalit*s are plunged into a pool of ignorance and superstitions. The story exposes the affected race of the *dalit*s as a consequence of illiteracy they turn a deaf ear towards mass education and therefore fall victim to the rampant *dalit*isation that occurs by taking the advantage of illiteracy. They are compelled to remain in the clutches of sorcerer. Even sometimes the situation turns so severe that they keep more faith in sorcerer than the doctors when Bhishnath's father suffers from terrible ache he never utters a word about the hospitals rather says,

> "hold me and carry me the bushes. I know the herbs and plants. You just grind the roots of herbs I identify and feed me the paste."

The lack of sense has a strong comment on the very *dalit* consciousness his father's indifference towards proper education seems to be got infiltrated in Bhishnath that bars him from taking his son suffering from high fever as he thinks.

"Which disease has been cured in the hospitals as yet."

This statement evidently evokes his ignorance but simultaneously the it also displays the degenerated condition of the hospitals which "knowing that the *dalit*s have no other way out but to go there" leads a diseased person to death. This lack of proper consciousness compels him to take the hasty decision of consulting Mangala to cure his son that led him to the consequent catastrophe following his son's painful death.

Following the great tragedy of his life Gharai brings out two very important outlook *dalit* consciousness: poverty and ignorance that is the scarcity of proper knowledge and education. The former is an integral part of *dalit*'s life as it becomes clear when Bhishnath's family faces constant scarcity of food, the very basic need when Madho falls ill.

"They could not light any lamp even after the previous night's rain and storm for want of Kerosene. Not only kerosene, everything in this village was scarce-rice, dal, makai atta, even edible wild roots and dried mahua"

The write in this story also exposes the fact that in our society, Gunins also are included among the powers that dominates over *dalit*s in the name of God and makes prices of *dalit*isation go unfairly rampant in society.

Mangala, the Gunin, not only economically exploits Bhishnath but also, poisons his mind. Influenced by his word Bhishnath kills his mother suspecting to be a witch that harms his son. His deeds lead him to a realisation of guilt when he finds his son dead after his mother's unwanted death.

Thus, the story has shown a completely different view if obstacles of a *dalit*'s life that force him to remain at the minimum level. Gharai gives a taste of salvation at last by the death of Mangala in Bhishanth's hand as the death of fears and drastic exploitations, the real witch of their life.

Nalini Bera's *Bara Bhaja, Kata Chokh o Badhuker Galpo* (Tr. *The Story of the Grey-eyed Oil-fry Seller*)

The Story of the Grey-eyed Oil-fry Seller is the translation of the 2003 Bengali story, *Bara Bhaja, Kata Chokh o Bankim Badhuker Galpo* which was published in Srestho Galpo: Nalini Bera has presented the readers almost a tear evoking grievous tale (or rather reality) of Parva Bisoi as to expose a natural phenomenon of superstitions in the rural areas that haunts the lives of destitute old woman with an explicit sense of indignation towards hatred disloyalty and betrayal from once decadence, that plays a mammoth part in the *dalit*ising a large amount of poor old persons brainlessly. The story has its narrators Nalini who, reminisces his past memories that encircles his friend Bankim, the village boys, an important examination, and most importantly Parva in a nostalgic mod and at the end gets despondent, finding out a sharp contrast between his past and the reality of the present. Parva, for all her affection towards Bankim, receives the reward in the form of getting beaten black and blue receiving the 'title' of a "witch" and at the same time complete alienation from the family. She had nurtured with all her heart. The story thus reflects the bitter truth of the reactions gone wrong as a result of some amiss and erroneous ideas of witchcraft that happens often in the remote areas even after passing and celebrating 70 years of Independence. Nalin Bera has appointed a wonderful narrative technique that never loses the local colour of the area he is describing.

The story gives vent to the villager's false notions on the presence of witchcraft that harms she lives of the poor woman as visual as also been echoed in Anil Gharai story, "Reincarnation of Parashuram."

In the introduction, the critic says,

> "the theme of ingratitude and betrayal of trust becomes quite apparent in the evolving relationship of Parva, the mother surrogate and Bankim Badhu, an ungrateful wretch."

Parva, who in spite of not being Bankim's biological mother finds the case of motherhood with her affection towards him, but at the end of the story Bankim throws her out of his house. Her complete isolation arouses sympathy in the reader's heart. A widowed woman, poor and helpless and can easily be regarded as a witch in a remote area. In the villages, not only in Midnapur but throughout West Bengal, the lack of proper education, plagues the areas, plunging them into dungeon of superstitions. In the very beginning of the story the narrator gives an account of witches he had seen in his childhood.

"I can remember Kamarburih (the old woman from the blacksmith family), Laitan's mother, Maliburih (the old woman whose name Malina was shorthened to Mali) and Barikh, all known witches."

It shows how time changes and nothing happens at all. The erroneous thoughts on witchcraft mainly in the marginalised society remains as it was in the days of narrator's childhood. As a result, woman like Parva is misjudged even committing no sin at all. This is the tragedy of our modern civilisation.

Taraknath Majhi's *Sakhya* (Tr. *Friendship*)

Friendship is the translation of the 1996 Bengali story *Shakhya* by Taraknath Majhi, published in Chaturthya Duniyar Galpo which provides us the opportunity of experiencing a unique narrative technique that is rich with a fervent psychological over tone, as well as the underlying rapid use and throw of common people that *dalit*ises and at the same time alienates them from the mainstream. The story has a strong comment on *Dalit* Consciousness that, at last proves the fact that in spite of having rivalry at youth, Gayanath and Majed Mian, a *dalit* and a *dalit* are actually into the same circle of immobility that has halted their previous glory as well as animosity irrespective of their racial variances. Gyanath dreams of his death and in the dream he himself makes all arrangements alone, indicating his alienation and utter helplessness., in the face of raging attacks of old age and insult. The author has, shown his mastery, by enabling the reader to have a pictorial effect of all incidents that go on rapidly. Gayanath, with a surging ache of superannuation finds him completely powerless in dream as well as in reality. Compared to him, his rival Majed Mian lives happily and content devoting himself to the spirituality even after losing his son. The theme apparently seems to be one day drawing of the life of a person, cursed with old age and depression but the underlying melancholy of the death and decay of thousands of people as a consequence of political agitation goes parallel with it. Gayanath has found flavour of friendship in his former enemy and at the same time faces strong and bitter reactions and responses from his near and dear ones like his daughter, in love. the story gives a faithful representation of the futility of expensive political theories and political parties that fails to produce any good impact on the real proletariats, the insignificance of the racial animosity as the title has mentioned has finally, the constant sufferings of poor man irrespective of the change of time and rule, even in democracy as in autocracy.

It is to be noted that Taraknath Majhi is not a familiar face in the field of *Dalit* literature like Anil Gharai rather an unknown personal who has tremendously made the story smell of intensity of the sufferings of a *dalit*ised individual. The critics have commented on the introduction,

> "in his story Shakhya (friendship) we notice the unravelling of a unique kind of consciousness. He has skilfully arranged the

> sequence of numerous political strives and conflicts in the Gangetic plains of West Bengal."

The story starts with a strange and at the same time very unique dream of Gayanath where he watches himself arranging for his death ceremony. Chopping woods and placing them in order over him to light a fire so that his body could be properly burnt. However, this Endeavour of him to make all arrangements alone even his death includes the underlying estrangement from human society as a result of old age in his subconscious mind. He had been of worth when he was young, and laboured a lot under the zamindar Mitra as a fighter. Time changed and vigorous youth burnt to make the ashes of old age. Now Gayanath is absolutely of no worth. His son and son's wife scorns him all the time,

> "can't you work and earn your living?"

It seems that the younger generation has rejected to recognise him as a part of society and has a somewhat dalitised him in spite of having a decent social recognition. Set in the backdrop of political agitation, and triumph of democracy, the story also attracts the attention of the readers to the very fact that the poor raging problem of political agitation. For every revolution, it demands loss of large amount of blood and what is a fact that the blood always sheds from a fragile body of the persons constantly suffering from poverty, who come to this field to fight only with a hope of a little bit of money and a land to live decently. Whether it is a twentieth century political theory of Marxism or age-old autocracy, no one, considers the price of a death of a poor person as a worth. Majed Mian, who later finds pace in spirituality on course of conversation avouches horrendously the bitter truth,

> "we were stick fighters in the days of the kings and zamindars and we are still stick fighters in the days of the party leaders...They used us and thrived that way."

The superiors in the social stature gives them worthwhile they have power in physique, and whenever they fail, getting old, they just mercilessly throw them away. The rapid *dalit*isation irrespective of caste and caste and social strata mainly based on wealth and worth has however broadened the very term "*dalit*" and simultaneously represented the helpless condition of the *dalit*s, in cruel hands of socio-political agitation and sudden change of authority, a universal catastrophe.

Manohar Mouli Biswas's *Munnali*

Munnali is a 1988 Bengali story by Manohar Mouli Biswas published in "Krishna Mrittikar Manush." In this tale, the translator has not changed the Bengali title of to restrain the very effect of the story. It is named after the main protagonist, Munnali, an adolescent with a huge hope of going out of the trash in which she is living. The life society provides her seems to the readers a hell, all her hopes lie on a specific Bishubabu who, though not actually present in the story, performs a very important role in bringing out the true nature of these kind of people. The entire story gives the readers a very brief description as well as consisting a very small plot, which ignites a light to give an honest scenario of India and oppressed ones. The story presents the two pictures which seem to be a bit awkward but at the same time true, Munnali, being a slum dweller cherishes a dream of seeing the light of the town of development but at last all hopes go ashtray as Bishubabu goes out and it becomes evident that he will never return there in any puja. Simultaneously, there is another incident that gives the reader a shock i.e. Munnali's father wants to her to marry with the son of Kanna Hella just because he is greater on caste. It shows how, Kansiram, Munnakli's father though being a part of racial discrimination, himself abides it by blindly without any proper reason. The author has taken up a brief slice of life just to show how a girl fells victim to a foul social system even now in this century. The narrative style and descriptions are honest and at the same time are examples of sheer prosaic art. The author has however shown his mastery by adding a beautiful line at the end,

> "Those who grow up in darkness look better with the ornaments of darkness."

As being a moral to the story it shows how frail, how fragile dreams are as it holds up the dreamers in air and it aches a lot when that "fragile" and somewhat "socially forbidden" dream ultimately breaks up smashing the dreamers in the firm ground.

In the introduction, critics have said about Munnali,

> "It is a touching tale of an individual who is cruelly reminded of the insurmountable social barrier even in modern times."

The story of Munnali makes the readers to give a close vigilance on the psychological and social condition of *dalits*. The story begins with a skyscraper dream of Munnali.

"I will not stay here. First, I will go to Kolkata, then cross Howrah bridge and go straight to Mumbai by catching a huge train…No I will not stay to this dirty hell of yours…not anymore. Just you see."

It shows how a poor girl is trying to get out of her dirty territory and gradually fighting against all her conditions but her dreams get suppressed by Nathuni Aunti in a harsh voice,

> "Oh! What day dreams! As if these babus will take a girl from the scavenging community and keep her as a cook in their homes."

The statement gives a great reflection of the mentality of the "Bhadrolok Babus" in the mirror of truth. They can give promises even knowing that they can't fulfil them. There is no place for the girl like Munnali in the city of civilised people. She is as if condemned, forbidden by the creel hands of society to enter in to the world of educated and polished. The story gives the reader the opportunity to look at themselves and contemplate on their psychological structure as determined by the society that inspires him to take part in the evil practice of racial discrimination and judge people according to their caste as well show pity with a sense of hatred towards the subalterns.

It seems as if society has created a strange barrier between Munnali and civilisation. As she is a slum dweller, as she is an epitome of poverty, she has no right to make dream of walking in the paths of a city with due honour. She wants to get out of darkness but nobody comes to her to bring her the light. Bishubabu doesn't even care if Munnali makes her way or not. It seems that he has done a great job by just showing her the dream, now he has no responsibility to help her to accomplish it.

Another aspect which is critical to *dalit* literature has popped out when Munnali's parents consult with each other about Munnali's marriage. In this conversation, the fact that Kanna Hella's other daughter in law has eloped with another man who was a cobbler by caste certainly comes out as an important cause for Kanna Hella, to make Munnali his daughter in law. Following the conversation, it should be taken critically that, how years from brainwash both from society and religion has made his false beliefs so firm that he even refuses to recognise Bhulo's son with whom she has eloped with, as a renowned one in spite of becoming affluent at last, just before being a *dalit*. This part of the story can be quoted as a proof to it,

> "Our Nathunui supplies hide to that shop and she says that Bhulo's son is like a prince. He has a thriving business which is blessed by Laxmi, the Goddess of wealth. Bhulo is not a cobbler anymore. The last sentence of his wife's speech irritated Kansiram. He looked sharply at his wife and burst out angrily, 'Not a cobbler anymore! What do you mean? Has he moved up in the caste-hierarchy? He tried to make out his wife's secret wishes and with a note of suspicion in his voice he asked, 'Are you planning to let our Munnali to be wedded into a cobbler's family?'" That is how throughout the entire story Munnali becomes a symbol, a face of a broken dream, of as number of women who cherish a dream but at last get forced to abandon it due to miserable circumstances. The ironical moral at the end evidently indicates the author's blatant announcement that society forbids the girls like Munnali to make a dream so big that she can't afford to touch even the feet of it.

Nakul Mallick's *Chashar Beta* (The *Son of a Peasant*)

The Son of a Peasant is the translation of the 2000 story written in Bengali, "Chashar Beta" by Nakul Mallik, published in Gram Ganjer Galpo that has the fragrance of the revolt of the people of the lower caste against their superiors who have undermined them so far. The main protagonist, Sudhanya Sarkar appears to be affluent but in fact, is an incarnation of a lower caste. He is an affluent and wealthy farmer, socially recognised as "Chandal", or "sudra". The people of the higher classes as the zamindar Moti Mukherjee, are used to humiliate and insult the lowers like Bishu Mondal. Years after years they have remained at the feet of the superiors. But the writer in this story has pointed out if these large crowd of people living at the dregs of the caste system are in majority, then why are they getting deliberately exploited by the people living in minority. This very question adds fire to their long-ago rage of being the "voiceless section of the society". Even the wealthy people like Sudhanya Sarkar have to face the same sort of humiliation while becoming a member of the managing committee of the school. Even he is bound within this territory. This enriches his consciousness and at the same time he becomes a face of the benumbed people. At the end of the story, it seems he has established justice in the heart of the diseased society which "Farmer Gopal's caste and creed" lacks. The writer seems to be had elicited the psychological structure that has so far barred the lower people with full of false notions about social hierarchy to revolt against their superiors but cannot hold for long. Sarkarmashai becomes a face of revolution and power of majority in the face of social hierarchy.

In the introduction part, critics have commented on the story,

> "*Chashar Beta* (*The Son of a Peasant*) by Nakul Mallik is a tale of Bold retaliation in order to establish justice. It is a vehement attack on the caste ridden psyche of society."

That explains the very theme of the story. Nakul Mallik has presented an optimistic view that executes his purpose to arouse *dalit* consciousness. Throughout the story, the traders are able to visualise a mammoth inequality as well as a sense of injustice to the people of the lower caste. At the very beginning of the story, Bishtu Mondal, gets rebuked with a reference of a "Chandal" for just walking with shoes on in the land of Gomostamashai of Khalia who belongs to a higher social caste and class.

> "take off your shoes and carry those in your hands while you walk at least in my fiefdom. You, son of a chandal, you think you have become a gentleman, you illiterate fellow, are you showing off like a babu?"

Even what is more pathetic the temple of learning the schools are schools are not free from the territory of social, positional, racial, hierarchy. The readers are able to watch and feel clearly the very social discrimination in the name of God., following Saraswati Puja in the high school of Khalia Village.

> "every year, Saraswati puja was organised in the school with great pomp. The students from Saramangal, South Khalia, Satpar and Kanaipur paid more subscriptions but they are denied the right to offer the Anjali sitting inside the pandal. They had to worship the Goddess standing outside and then go away just taking the Prasad. This had been a matter for concern for everybody for quite a long time, but there was scarcely anybody to lead a protest."

All these incidents show the beguiled social exploits of the people of lower caste, irrespective of their wealth or education by the well-established people un social and caste hierarchy.

However, the endeavour of Sudhanya, to put a stop to all that shadows of injustice, can be regarded praiseworthy as it was next to impossible in such a socio economical ambience. The author has shown a light of revolution among the *dalits*.

The way Sudhanya Sarkar makes the unruly, insulting zamindar, Moti Majumdar, his "bullock", to give him a lesson is laced with his immense hatred towards the persons like him.

"Sarkarmashai ordered "drag that gentleman, son of a gentleman and bind him to the yoke."

The story can be regarded as completely exceptional from all the other stories as other stories expose only the miserable hostilities of their life while this story becomes an ideal of the *dalit* revolt.

Society always undermines and exploits them, but what if, one day, they get agitated and fight back against them? This story brings out the fore of their constant sufferings in the form of establishing equality and justice.

4

Conclusion

"Man is the centrifugal force in the philosophy of dalit literature. Man is supreme. He is above Gods, sacred books and science."

Tarachand Khandekar.

The phrase that demands mammoth exposure inside the sphere of contemporary creative arts like literature is obviously, nothing other than, "*dalit* literature", which has retained its existence so far amidst massive suppression by the other "aristocratic" or rather "posh" sectors of literary endeavors. This specific genre has a completely different appeal to the readers who are tired of going through too embroidered, artificial and myriad superficial style of writing that in many ways present a stream of either scattered or forcefully bound up complex ideas. Unlike these innumerable techniques that beguile the readers mind by presenting hypothetical realities only to make them fall into the dungeon of isolation from the reality, *dalit* literature, with its humble, rustic and "to the point" narrative style enforces the reader to make his voyage through stern reality as faced by the "voiceless section of the society". The word "*dalit* literature" is so multidimensional that it paves the way towards countless forms and faces of literature like poetry, short story, essays, autobiographies and even speeches.

The very origin of the term "minority writer" takes us back to the grainy past when the dark-complexioned mass from Africa and other countries of darkness were traded as slaves, their hands and feet tied up (cementing the possibility of their existential crisis) and transported towards America by the white race of the original

American Indians. Numerically the "white" countries were abounding in "black" slaves; therefore, judged by the statistical account of the mass, these people could hardly be called a minority. The point of their forceful alienation from the "civilised" zone of society was not religion but this was based on their skin color that they were deliberately been a subject to hatred, oppression and physical assault. When the light of education touched their entity, the scenario came to a radical change. In 1993 Toni Morrison won the Nobel Prize for literature and identified herself as a "minority writer" in front of the media. This "black writer" claiming her to be a minority writer opens before us a wide vista of social spectrum. With this, the new genre of literature flourished itself as a matter of discourse and research.

The term "*Dalit*" takes its origin from the Sanskrit verb "dal" (to divide) and of late the term that literally means adjectives such as, "divided, split, broken, scattered etc." has diversified connotations to different individuals. The Marxists however mean by the term, the rabble generally seen as "economically backward", no matter what their caste identity is. For Hardtmann who imposes a separate thought demarcates it as,

> "An ethnic concept referring to people who use it self-ascribingly. (Hardtmann IX)"

However, from a general point of view, the term demarcates a large group of socially oppressed people in India. The emphasis is given upon the group's social exclusion as they were proclaimed "untouchables" by the law givers of traditional Hindu "Varna" system. In India, *dalit* writing has a pan-Indian spread. Minority writing has already created a minor revolution in almost every Indian state, among people of different linguistic groups.

Dalit literature has arisen from basically cultural conflict. In the words of Bahurao Bagul,

> "...it is *Dalit* literature which has the revolutionary power to accept new science and technology and bring about a total transformation. "*Dalit*" is the name of a total revolution; it is revolution incarnate."

That combats with the very fact that the 'downtrodden' has no place or hardly any place in the canonical literature of India.

Unlike the non-*dalit*s, the *dalit* writers remain completely truthful about their day-to-day life experience with all their existence of flesh and blood without any veil of euphemism. This marks another important feature of *dalit* literature that though the language, diction and descriptions of them are mostly in an undistilled raw manner, often using brutal and coarse language of the slum dwellers, they remain as a faithful account of their life springing from poverty, ignorance and exploitation.

These sheer pieces of literature have always a notion or rather assonance to a revolt of the people smelling of raw sweat which has always worked as an inspiration for them.

In this pan-Indian scenario, these minority writers have spread from *Mahar*ashtra (where it started), Gujarat, Karnataka, and Punjab to West Bengal, Tripura, Assam and Meghalaya too. They have inculcated themselves into the annals of the Bengali literature. The movement to declare their separate existence in the 1960s has now spread across the whole subcontinent. The interesting fact about this form is that at its heart lies "reform" clad in the attire of art.

Among the other forms of *dalit* craftsmanship, short story has now days reached at its zenith due to a number of *dalit* litterateurs who have shown their effort to portray the glimpses of their daily struggle for existence. This form has come to light mainly because of the several opportunities that it conceives.

According to Wikipedia,

> "A short story is a piece of prose fiction that can be read in one sitting. Emerging from earlier oral storytelling traditions in the 17th century, the short story has grown to encompass a body of work so diverse as to defy easy characterisation. At its most prototypical the short story features a small cast of named characters, and focuses on a self-contained incident with the intent of evoking a "single effect" or mood. In doing so, short

> stories make use of plot, resonance, and other dynamic components to a far greater degree than is typical of an anecdote, yet to a far lesser degree than a novel. While the short story is largely distinct from the novel, authors of both generally draw from a common pool of literary techniques."

It is evident that short story is a form that is too much appealing for everyone. Unlike poetry or novel or drama, it can be enjoyed anytime anywhere. This very opportunity has increased its value and importance amongst all sorts of readers and non-readers. It is true indeed that a short story is a piece of prose fiction that can be completed in a single reading. Unlike other forms it does not need to be analysed much and it does not need more than a week to conclude up. The short story is usually concerned with a single effect displayed in only one or a few significant episodes or scenes. The form encourages several points like economy of setting, concise narrative, and the omission of a complex plot; character is disclosed in action and dramatic encounter but is seldom fully developed. Despite its relatively limited scope, though, a short story is often judged by the ability to provide a "complete" or satisfying treatment of its characters and subject. The point of view of a short story is indeed interesting and a point to be noted. Point of view is the camera angle from which the writer presents the story. In first-person point of view, "I" is used, and the narrator is typically a character involved in the story. In the second person (the least used point of view), you is used, in an effort to make the reader a character. In third-person, the narrator is a voice external to the story, using he or she in relating events. Point of view can be limited (allowing no access to characters' thoughts), omniscient (allowing access to all characters' thoughts) or semi-omniscient (allowing access to the thoughts of selected characters).

In the postcolonial period, this genre called "short story" flourished to a great extent and gave vent to several new aspects of society. One of the important causes for this is obviously, it represents most prominently their problematised identities than the other forms or style of writing. The different and traumatic experiences in the colonial time and its ruptures are spoken out through its short story especially focusing on several themes like self, identity and nation. It probably is the aftermath of a wide discourse about the colonial period or it may not be a deliberate attempt. But the themes and their significance with the age strengthen the bedrock of the short story. It is quite visible in almost all colonies and post colonies. But it does not mean that short story is the only suitable or amenable genre to the postcolonial backdrop; but ought to say that its influence cannot be negligible.

The obvious question, that has risen after much time has flown away, whether short story be included into the sphere of 'minor literature' or not mainly takes its origin from the opinions of Gilles Deleuze and Felix Guattari in their study, "Kafka: Toward a Minor Literature" (1975). They define the minor literature as the "writing which a minority constructs within a major language" (Hunter 139). So, it is evident that, minor literature occurs in language which is de-territorialised or displaced (it may through colonisation) and it is this displacement which fits the language for strange and minor uses. It is debatable if the short story can be part of Minor Literature, but it can be an instrument of it if the writers want to express in that way.

According to Limbale,

> "If *Dalit* literature appears to be propagandist, it is because it presents the *Dalit* writers" anguish and their questions...*Dalit* writers cannot sever their relationships with pain...the questions they pose in their work are their own, and those of their society...intense lived and felt experiences cannot be called propagandist." (Limbale 34)

It is a fact indeed that like the caste discrimination *dalit* literature, mainly *dalit* short stories has a stigma attached to it, that it is the literature of the oppressed. It has always stood in sharp contrast with the traditional literature, which often makes these stories as resentful, propagandist, univocal and monotonous. But it also makes another feature of the *dalit* short stories. Moreover, these stories mainly center round a single character and take up a single incident from his/her life and attribute universal significance and importance to it. These features can be illustrated from various short stories taken from *Survival and Other Stories* and *Poisoned Bread*, the former deals with the life of the *dalit*s in Bengal while the latter exposes the reality of *Mahar*ashtra.

Survival and Other Stories is a collection of short stories edited by Sankar Prasad Singha and Indranil Acharya containing several works like, The Deceived, Footprint of an Elephant, Reincarnation of Parashuram, The Sky of Draught, Bazaar, On Water and on Shore, On Firm Ground etc.

The Deceived by Achintya Biswas is the very first story that has a bulky frame and for that reason scarcely we can call it a short story if judged by its size. The story has a complex narrative and deals with a number of characters but mainly places its focus on two *dalit* individuals: Gopal and Maya. The story exposes the shabby treatment of the *dalit* individuals and suppressions over them by the authority and administration as well as the hypocrisy of the political leaders and the progressive intellectuals who turn a deaf ear to the actual nauseating scenario and avouch with pride that the curse of untouchability has left West Bengal forever. The fate of the people like Golap who try to protest is predestined to be dead without any medical supervision that he requires. When Maya in the form of Mahamaya, tried to protest against the caste system by speaking out that she will drink their blood, the two corrupt, high-caste person, Nilu and Anamay sent goons to the temple where Gopal and Maya resided and they cut the beard and matted hair of Gopal, trying to prove his futility of spirituality and what is more pathetic, brutally raped her (Maya). The story has vehemently dealt with the sensitive portions of the story and has raised itself to the level of a short story with its abrupt ending and singleness of theme: caste discrimination.

Footprints of an Elephant has a different approach which deals with mainly the tragic life of Bhima and Bishahari. The very word "elephant" serves as a symbol of destruction that becomes clear at the end of the story when Bishahari draws the footprint of evil Jata instead of an elephant on the ground. Rampant sexual exploitation of the *dalit* individuals by the superiors and their helplessness before the supreme is made clear in the story via Bishahari's story and Bhima, who becomes an element of the evil deeds of Jata just to fulfill his hunger. The story has a brief body and the story jas the unity of setting, plot and characters.

Reincarnation of Parashuram deals with a completely different subject matter, "superstition" that mars the development of the downtrodden people. The myth of Parashuram in the oriental text has been implemented fruitfully inside the character of Bhisnath Barlar who kills his mother following the "judgement" of the "gunin" Mangala thinking her to be a witch trying to kill his son Madho. This very fact gives a tight slap in the face of the superstitions and is carried forward by the death of Madho and finally, the killing of Mangala in the hands of Bhisnath. The story is one of Anil Gharai's most renowned ones that deals with the two aspects of a *dalit* individual: poverty and ignorance which is illustrated throughout the narrative that has a keen insight into the subaltern life with all its beliefs and lack of proper education.

The Sky of Draught is also another important work of Anil Gharai that has shown how helpless a man is when he is forced to consume a dog-bitten swine and meet utter hostilities in his life. Nuna Mandi, the protagonist of the story faces a somewhat "psycho-economical" crisis following poverty and his pregnant wife that end up in a hospital getting saline water in his body as life. Most importantly, the story is made the two words "sky" and "draught" seek for a universal appeal and rightly employed to denote the society and life of a helpless *dalit* individual. Moreover, the abrupt ending and almost poetic endeavor amidst the story has given the story a different dimension.

Bazaar by Gautam Ali is perhaps the most tabooed story regarding the *dalit*s where several *dalit* women are getting exploited and muted by their superior masters. The village girl who comes at the house of a wealthy person as a household help is forced to "submit to the libidinal demands of her middle-aged upper-class employer." The story shows a woman's several attempts to hold their own position in society and as a means of it, the victimisation of several poor woman in the hands of a husband's lascivious nature forms the very eye-catching realistic outlook towards a rotten society where women are nothing but benumbed creatures.

The story *On Water and on Shore*, has a strong comment on *Dalit* Consciousness that follows the footsteps of the fisherman Shashi. While in this story, Shashi fails to protest against Nagenbabu who betrayed him and ends up the conversation with Nagen Sharma by a meager "Hmm", Haladhar, becomes a face of revolt against the Brahmins in "On Firm Ground", only to end up in the realisation, "Wasn't there an inch of earth in this wide world on which they could safely stand?"

The Other Jew is a tale that takes us back to the era of the turbulent '71. The migrants after the partition lie at the center of the story who became a nobody either it is India or East Pakistan. The story is a soul searing comment on the helplessness of a disadvantaged group at the tentative mercy of callous political parties and their goons. The tragic fate of Bishtucharan only cements the concept of rapid *dalit*isation of a stormy time. The story has a lot of actions but its tragic mood and loyal account of the incidents, takes it to the level of an ideal frame of a short story.

The three stories that has a very tiny frame is *Farmer Gopal's Caste and Creed*, *Munnali* and *Shabori* deal with the three diversified topics which are equally appealing and important to open up the blind eyes of the society. The first one deals with a *dalit* individual's endeavor to find a means to earn money and at last his refusal to give the pond to the government. It has an optimistic note that, rampant *dalit*isation of have-nots have somehow one way or the other succeeded to diminish the caste related or racial ego among the *dalit*s themselves. The second story is a tear-evoking tale of the broken dream of a little girl; Munnali who had dreamt of going out to the big city and live her life there. The third one deals with a more heart-breaking notion; the sexual exploitation of Padma, a "shabori" which comes out quite ironically in the words of her; "Babu, it is because of us that decent woman can walk freely." All the three stories have the paucity of characters and a poetic mood that casts a spell around the reader and enforces him to walk his way through the hurdle some reality that these subalterns are gifted with.

The Son of a Peasant is a comparably long story that ends with a sense of optimism. It has the fragrance of the revolt of the people of the lower caste against their superiors who have undermined them so far. The spirit of revolution that gets defeated in *On Firm Ground*, tastes victory in the story via the revolt of Sudhanya Sarkar who being a peasant by caste succeeds to punish the Brahmins. However, the story teaches indirectly the necessity of a revolution among the *dalits*.

Though the plot of the story *The Story of the Grey-eyed Oil Fry seller* is much loose than the rest of the stories, it also has a completely different effect upon the psyche of the readers. The story speaks of the miserable plight of Parva Bisoi and her unconditional love towards her favorite chap Bankimo, while the misconceptions and superstitions about witches and witchcraft prevailing rampant in the *dalit* community. Based on the remembrance of the narrator Nalini, the story echoes the same theme as seen in *Reincarnation of Prashuram*, though the subject matter and the contents are completely different; "Witches and witchcraft! All nonsense! All superstitions! As simple as that!"

Survival by Shyamal Kumar Pramanik deals with the intense ache of a hungry stomach that breaches the difference between a man and a beast. The story shows how "rationality" gets removed from human qualities if he is deprived from one of his basic needs; "food." Raju, the protagonist of the story goes that far to snatch food and fight with a ferocious snake in order to get food. But the story ends with a sense of optimism as finally he succeeds to get food from that hole for him and his family. This shows however the brutality of man under excessive *dalit*isation. The story is written in a lucid manner with flashbacks into his childhood with the wonderful portrayal of characters.

Dhani Bauri Gets Salvation starts with a very relevant and necessary interrogation regarding *dalit* consciousness: "Why don't they get social acceptance even when they spent the entire Baishakh month uttering "Haribol"?" The story exposes the unconditional mother-like love of Dhani Bauri towards Hiru Majhi, as seen in the other story, *The Story of the Grey-eyed Oil Fry Seller"* and end up in insult. The very word "salvation" is identical to get Ganges as the holy river is believed to preserve and ornamented seat in heaven after someone's death in Hindu mythology. The title indirectly indicates that it is quite unnatural for the untouchable woman like Dhani Bauri to get salvation. The story has evoked even a more dangerous thing, i.e., the caste hierarchy even among the *dalit* communities.

Mukunda and an Extraordinary Love Affair has presented a completely different flavor in order to show the love affair between two young lovers, breaking their caste identity, emitting the odor of humanism all over. The very Mahasweta Gram performs as a location where all the incidents of this story take place. The writer has evidently spoken of our heart and has found the definition of true education. The story however is full of Mukunda's thoughts and experiences. The story contains all that is needed to make a story truly spectacular in the eyes of the readers. The title has spoken of an "extraordinary" love affair which serves as the main and most interesting part of the story. Susnata Jana, the writer has depicted a story that has touched our heart.

The last two stories *Friendship* and *Fisherman* has a very small plot and brief frame but something important gets exposed all through the stories. While the former avouches, that in spite of having rivalry at youth, Gayanath and Majed Mian, a *dalit* and a *dalit* are actually into the same circle of immobility that has halted their previous glory as well as animosity irrespective of their racial variances., the latter announces the ultimate sense of unity and oneness among fishermen, no matter what their caste identity or religious identity is, "As long as we are on water, we have one caste-that of fisherman."

The book entitled *The Poisoned Bread* contains short stories such as, *The Poisoned Bread*, *The Storeyed House*, Explosion etc.

The Poisoned Bread undoubtedly makes out the eternal oppression of the *Mahar*s by the Patils or the land lords. The tear evoking tale of Yetalya and his grandson Mhadeva present the scenario crystal clear that no matter how educated the *Mahar*s be, they will have to remain under the feet of the land lords. The "poisonous bread" that caused the death of Yetalya becomes a symbol itself of the anger of the minority crowds, mainly the educated grandson, Mhadeva. The story is written in a way that it presents the readers the twofold feelings; pathos and awareness, two important elements of *dalit* consciousness that need to be illustrated via short stories.

The Storeyed House by Waman Hoval is a story that too, exposes the miserable plight of the *Mahar*s. The dream of building a new storeyed house by Bayaji ends up in ashes. The author has used a terrific narrative technique that evokes pathos in a very different manner.

Explosion speaks of the pain of unemployment of an educated young *dalit*, Shetiba, who is getting forced to commit scavenging for money. The story has a really pathetic end where Shetiba goes out of the house even in high fever to get a job. The immense curse of hunger, poverty and the fruitless education that mars the *Promotion* of the working class has been depicted vehemently by the author, Yogiraj Waghmare.

Promotion by Arjun Dangle is the story that has exposed the most complex and psychological conflict of a person, Waghmare who could not determine what his real caste identity is, on one hand he wants to retain his status but on the other hand the humiliation over his son gives him the clear implication that the *dalit*isation is like an epidemic that spreads all over from the uneducated spectrum to the educational and occupational sphere.

"Livelihood" speaks of poverty and sexual exploitation. What should a poor woman do when she is dying of dire poverty? This very question makes the theme of the story, the very word "livelihood" has been universalised here in order to show the cry of a *dalit* mother. The society produces only unemployment to the working class and therefore they become goons, thieves, murderers and get forced to choose the crooked line. On the other hand, it also shows the miserable and helpless state of the poor marginalised women of the society that they get forced to choose the occupation of prostitution to earn their livelihood. The story is undoubtedly the one which produces versatile effects on the reader's psyche, a very unique characteristic of a short story.

Mother by Baburao Bagul discusses a very sensitive matter regarding the exploitation of a poor *dalit* widow not only in the hands of her high caste overseer, but also in the hands of her own husband and the society. The final blow comes when she is misunderstood even by her own son. It has the smell of patriarchy prevalent in the marginalised communities. Thus, becomes evident by statements such as, "your sari looks as if you've won it in a hurry, your hair's coming loose, where were you, slut?" With her husband's death, she has become an object of enjoyment to every male, from her overseer to her neighbor Dagdu. The ending that Bagul offers to his readers is symbolic of the eternal oppression that the *dalit* women face and from where their release is indeed impossible. This creates the tragic mood of the story. Her son only gets insult and punishment due to casteism. This boundary and its consequence find a better expression in the story: "She was trying desperately to escape from the bear-like hug of the overseer. But like a person stuck fast in a quagmire, she found release impossible …"

The short story of Amitabh, *The Cull* points out two important sides of hunger-stricken persons: inhuman desire (almost beast like) for food and helpless condition. The end that Nilya faces evidently expresses what he is going to get at his house for food. The immense hunger of the entire *Mahar* community shows also the lack of food that leads them to live the life of an animal.

Barriers brings out the exploitation of Zingu who belongs to the so-called low caste, *Mahar*. Zingu is firm in his decision of sending his only son, Narayan Zingroji Zende to Murtijapur to continue his studies further at Janata High School where he is ill-treated and humiliated for being an untouchable. At last, Narayan quits the school and burns the headmaster, Dongre's house along with him. By doing this, he thinks that as if he burns untouchability itself. This very point makes clear the necessity of a revolt of the *dalit* youths for proper education two drive away the curse of untouchability.

Another story entitled *Gold from the Grave* written by Anna Bhau Sathe reveals that how a man from *Dalit* society digs graves to find out gold which is buried along with the dead bodies. A man from a village strays over to big city like Bombay but there he finds nothing, this shows the dire unemployment of *Dalit*. Being compelled by circumstances, he adopts grave digging as his profession. But accidently, one day he loses his fingers in this profession. The story gives focuses the way which a man has to follow in order to make his bare survival.

In the story *The Refugee* by Avinash Dolas the twenty-one years old boy "tried to come to grips with the turmoil in his mind and turned to look back just once. But the village was out of sight. The trees and the bushes had obliterated it. It was as if nothing had happened." The boy has become a refugee in his own land. In the railway station, he thinks himself to be a dog. This is the *dalit* reality expressed in this story. So, Ambedkar says, "Gandhiji, I have no homeland."

It is to be said that in the light of the continuing practice of untouchability, and increasing incidents of the inhuman crimes against *dalit*s the very word that is perhaps more necessary to focus on; "awareness." These short stories unlike the novel, do not give us narrative constitutes, but rather instances. The *dalit* writers, whether it is about the scenario of Bengal or the *Mahar*astra, whether it is the *sudra*s or the *mahar*s deliberately point out showing their mastery, the tragic plight of the persons of the soil. The condensed form of the short story has distinctively succeeded to produce more grief evoking effect as well as the anger of revolt in the mind of the readers. The 'deaths' in the stories examined here do not display a celebration of the fragmented subject, but a hush, a mourning, a constructed act of remembrance of those who do not 'make it' into the temples of modern progress. At last, the readers are only left to end up following the words of Neerav Patel in his poem, "Anguish",

> "this is the ultimatum
> written in terrorist ink by a dalit poet
> – the kali incarnated"

Select Bibliography

Primary Sources

Dangle, Arjun (Ed.). P*oisoned Bread, Modern Marathi & Dalit Literature* (Tr.) New Delhi, Orient BlackSwan Pvt. Ltd, 2009.

Prasad Singha, Sankar and Acharya, Indranil (Eds.). *Survival and other stories: Bangla Dalit fiction in translation*, New Delhi, Orient Blackswan, 2012.

Secondary Sources

Moon, Vasant. *Growing up Untouchable in India*, Lanham, MD, Rowman & Little, 2000.

Bama, Karukku. Chennai, Macmillan India, 2000.

Eagleton, Terry. 'History, narrative, and Marxism', in James Phelan (ed.), Reading Narrative: form, ethics, ideology, Columbus, Ohio University Press, 1989.

Marx, Karl. *Selected Writings*, Oxford, Oxford University Press, 1977; ed. David McLellan.

Zelliot, Eleanor. *From Untouchable to Dalit: essays on the Ambedkar movement,* New Delhi, Manohar, 1992.

B. R. Ambedkar, *Writings and Speeches* (Mumbai, Government of Maharashtra, 1979-98; ed. Vasant Moon)

Omvedt, Gail. *Dalits and the Democratic Revolution: Dr Ambedkar and the Dalit movement in colonial India*, New Delhi, Sage, 1994.

Hardiman, David. *Gandhi: In His Times and Ours.* Delhi: Permanent Black, 2003.

Ramachandran, Shalini. "'Poisoned Bread': protest in Dalit Short Stories," *Sage Journal,* Issue published on April 1, 2004.

Justin, Jovita. "Under the Yoke: Representation of the Class Struggle in Select Dalit Fiction," *Veda's Journal of English Language and Literature* (JOELL), Vol. 3 Issue 1, 2016.

Prasad Singha, Sankar and Acharya, Indranil (Eds.). *Towards Social Change: Essays on Dalit Literature*, New Delhi, Orient Blackswan, 2014.

Coward, Harold, *Indian Critiques of Gandhi*, SUNY Press, 2012.

Nayar, Pramod K. *The Poetics of Postcolonial Atrocity: Dalit Life Writing, Testimonio, and Human Rights*, Ariel, 2012. Web.

Singh, Omendra Kumar, "Reinventing Caste: Indian Diaspora in Amitav Ghosh's Sea of Poppies," ASIATIC, 2012. Web.

Sarangi, Jaydeep, Editor's Note: Issue 46, *Muse India Archives*, 2012. Web.

Agarwal, B.R. "Subaltern Concerns in the Novels of Mulk Raj Anand" *in Mulk Raj Anand*. Ed. B.R. Agarwal. New Delhi: Atlantic, 2006.

Ambedkar, B.R. *Annihilation of Castes with a Reply to Mahatma Gandhi*. Bombay, Bharatbhusan Printing Press, 1946.

Ambedkar, B.R. *Thus Spoke Ambedkar: Selected Speeches*. Ed. by Bhagwan Das, Jullundur, Bheem Patrika Publications, 1969.

Anand, Mulk Raj. "On the Genesis of Untouchable" in *The Novels of Mulk Raj Anand*. Ed. R. K. Dhawan. New Delhi: Prestige, 1992.

Bandyopadhyay, Jayantanuja. *Social and Political Thought of Gandhi*. Howrah: Manuscript India, (1969) 2000.

Chakrabarty, Dipesh. "A Small History of Subaltern Studies." *A Companion to Postcolonial Studies*. Eds. Henry Schwarz and Sangeeta Ray. Malden: Blackwell, 2000. 467-85.

Chowdhury, Kanishka. "Transnational Transgressions: Reading Mira Nair's *Kama Sutra*and Deepa Mehta's Fire in a Global Economy." *South Asian Review: Globalisation and Diaspora*. Ed. K.D. Verma.Vol. 24. Johnstown: U of Pittsburgh, 2003. 180-201.

Dasgupta, Sayantan. "Dalit writing in Bangla: Repression and Resistance in ManiranjanByapari and ManjuBala's Narratives." *Jadavpur Journal of Comparative Literature*, No. 46, 2008-9. pp. 110-125

Devy, G. N. (Translated) Limbale, Sharankumar. "Chronicle of a Fatherless Being". *A. Ba. Ka. Da. I*, Diwali Special Number 1986.

Dirks, Nicholas B. *Castes of Mind: Colonialism and the Making of Modern India*. Princeton and Oxford: Princeton UP, 2001.

Franco, Fernando, "Jyotsna Macwan and Suguna Ramanathan." *Journeys to Freedom: Dalit Narratives.* Kolkata: SAMYA, 2004.

Freeman, Mark. "Charting the Narrative Unconscious: Cultural Memory and the Challenge of Autobiography". *Narrative Inquiry*, 12:1, 2002, pp. 193-211.

Gandhi, M.K. *An Autobiography or The Story of my Experiences with Truth.* Ahmedabad: Navajivan Trust, 1996(1927).

Gandhi, M.K. *The Removal of Untouchability.* Ahmedabad: Navjivan Publishing House, 1954.

Gupta, Sonya Surabhi. "Miguel Barnet's Biography of a Runaway Slave: Revisiting 'Testimonio' from Dalit-Caliban Vantage Point." *Jadavpur Journal of Comparative Literature*, No. 46, 2008-9. pp. 74-87.

Hardiman, David. *Gandhi: In His Times and Ours.* Delhi: Permanent Black, 2003.

Hardtman, Eva-Maria. *The Dalit Movement in India: Local Practices, Global Connections.* New Delhi: Oxford University Press, 2009.

Hari, A. Jaganmohana. "Óutside the Magic Circle: A Study of Anand's Untouchable" in *The Novels of Mulk Raj Anand: A Critical Study,* Ed. Manmohan K. Bhatnagar and M. Rajeshwar. New Delhi: Atlantic, 2000.

Ilaiah, Kancha. *Why I am not a Hindu: A Sudra Critique of Hindutva Philosophy, Culture and Political Economy. Calcutta: SAMYA,* 1996.

Indra Mohan, T.M.J. *The Novels of Mulk Raj Anand: A New Critical Spectrum.* New Delhi: Atlantic, 2005.

Kamble, Ramesh. "Untouchability in Urban Setting: Everyday Social Experiences of Ex-Untouchables in Bombay" in Ghanshyam Shah (ed.), *Dalits and the State.* New Delhi: Concept Publishing, 2002.

Kumar, Gajendra. "Untouchable: A Manifesto of Indian Socio-Political Realism"in *The Novels of Mulk Raj Anand: A Critical Study.* Ed. Manmohan K.

Bhatnagar and M. Rajeshwar. New Delhi, *Atlantic,* 2000.

Lal, A. C. 'Foreword' *in Dalit Solidarity* (ed.) Bhagwan Das and James Massey. Delhi: ISPCK, 1995.

Limbale, Sharankumar. *The Outcaste: Akkarmashi.* Translated from Marathi by Santosh Bhoomkar. New Delhi: Oxford University Press, 2008.

Limbale, Sharankumar. *Towards an Aesthetic of Dalit Literature: History, Controversies and Considerations.* Translated by Alok Mukherjee. New Delhi: Orient Longman, 2004.

Lloyd, David. "Ethnic Cultures, Minority Discourse and the State." *Colonial Discourse/ Postcolonial Theory.* Eds. Francis Barker, Peter Hulme and Margaret Iversen. Manchester: Manchester UP, 1994. 221-38.

Mitchell, W.J.T. "Representation" in Critical Terms for Literary Study" (2nd ed.), edited by Frank Lentricchia and Thomas McLaughlin, Chicago: University of Chicago Press, 1997.

Mukherjee, Arun Prabha. "Introduction" in Omprakash Valmiki, *Joothan: A Dalit's Life.* English translation. Kolkata: Samya, 2007.

Mukherjee, Prabhati. *Beyond the Four Varnas: The Untouchables in India.* Shimla, Indian Institute of Advanced Study, 1988.

Nigam, N.M. "Mulk Raj Anand: A Messiah of the Poor and the Downtrodden" in *Mulk Raj Anand,* Ed. B.R. Agarwal. New Delhi: Atlantic, 2006.

Poitevin, Guy. "Dalit Autobiographical Narratives: Figures of Subaltern Consciousness, Assertion and Identity." http://aune.1pl.univaix.fr/~belbernard/misc/ccrss//Dalitautobio.htm (Accessed on June 6, 2009)

Prasad, HariOm. "Mulk Raj Anand's Coolie: A Saga of Suffering" in *The Novels of Mulk Raj Anand: A Critical Study,* Ed. Manmohan K. Bhatnagar and M. Rajeshwar. New Delhi: Atlantic, 2000.

Sadangi, H.C. *Emancipation of Dalits and Freedom Struggle,* Delhi: Isha Books, 2008.

Sarma, Rani Siva Sankara. *The Last Brahmin.*Translated from the Telugu by D. VenkatRao.Ranikhet: Permanent Black, 2007.

Shah, Ghanshyam, (ed.). *Dalits and the State.* Mussoorie; Centre for Rural Studies, Lalbahadur Shastri National Academy of Adminstration, 2002.

Shukla, R.N. "Mulk Raj Anand: A Tribute" *in Mulk Raj Anand,* Ed. B.R. Agarwal. New Delhi: Atlantic, 2006.

Spivak, Gayatri Chakravorty "Can the Subaltern Speak?" Columbia University Press, 2010.

Suleri, Sara. *The Rhetoric of English India.* Chicago and London: University of Chicago Press, 1992.

Tripathy, Revati Ballav. *Dalits: A Sub-Human Society*. New Delhi: Ashish Publishing, 1994.

Valmiki, Omprakash. *Joothan: A Dalit's Life.* Translated from Hindi by Arun Prabha Mukherjee. Kolkata: Samya, 2007.

Index